THE CHRISTMAS CONVENT CHILD

A WARM PUREREAD CHRISTMAS

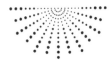

DOLLY PRICE

© 2020 PUREREAD LTD

PUREREAD.COM

CONTENTS

CHAPTER ONE

LIVERPOOL 1870

"Whey we going?" The little girl did not know why Bridie was putting her bonnet on her this late in the day. And Bridie was different today. She wasn't singing or playing with her.

"Whey Mamma?"

Bridie bit back her tears as she made the little girl ready to go to her Uncle and Aunt's house.

"She'll be here when we come back," she said, knowing that Eliza would never return.

Downstairs, the maid Julia went to answer the doorbell. It was a loud and impatient sound but then the Mercers were loud and impatient people. She did not like them. Her friend Sarah worked for them for a while and she said they were the most tight-fisted people she'd ever known and she'd known plenty. She was leaving as soon as she got another position.

The Mercers almost knocked Julia down in their haste to get in.

"Where were you? Is she ready?"

"Yes, Bridie is just … "

"Where is she then?"

"Upstairs, Bridie is nearly …"

"What's the delay? We haven't all evening to stand about! You said you'd send over the house keys. If you had, we wouldn't have to stand on the doorstep in the rain!"

"Richard has the keys, Mr. Mercer. I will fetch Miss Elizabeth." Julia departed up the stairs, but did not hurry herself, to spite them.

"Richard! The keys of the house!" bellowed the visitor, only he did not consider himself a visitor now. This house belonged to the child, and he was the child's guardian.

The last few days had been a nightmare for the small staff of the pleasant house on Knotty Ash, ever since they'd heard of the accident, the sailboat that sank on the Mersey. Their young cheerful Master and their kind, beautiful Mistress had been drowned. They had wept a great deal. Little Eliza was an orphan at three years old, and their hearts broke for her, because her uncle and aunt now had guardianship - and control of the little heiress' wealth.

"It's like throwing a kitten to hungry wolves," Julia had said bitterly. "I'm sorry she wasn't with her Ma and Pa, and she would've been, only for the sniffles, she might have been better off."

"Don't say that," Bridie had said, blessing herself. "God will look after the wee one. I know I'm going to put her in my daily prayers. Will you?"

"If it wasn't for you, Bridie, I would have lost all hope for the world. Yes, I'll pray for her too. But as for that being an accident - you should get your brother to look into it, you should."

"Sean only began in the Force last week Julia! He barely knows his way to the Parade Ground!"

The servants were now out of work, as this house was to be shut down and sold. Only Bridie was asked to remain in the service of Elizabeth's guardians. Mrs. Mercer had engaged her not out of any consideration for the child but because if there were difficulties, tears and tantrums, Bridie would know how to deal with them. She had not employed a nursery maid for many years. Their family was grown. Their eldest son Theo ran a plantation in Jamaica, their daughter Millicent was married in Malta, and they were not on speaking terms with the youngest, George.

As the carriage rattled along the crowded streets, Bridie held Elizabeth in her lap, her arms wrapped about her. She had fallen asleep with her thumb in her mouth.

I don't know how long I'm going to be able to bear working for these people, she thought, *but I'll try to stay until Eliza is settled and happy. I pray that will happen soon! Maybe the old woman over there will get fond of her after all and take her mamma's place.* But her hopes evaporated when Mrs. Mercer opened her mouth to address her husband.

"What is the house worth, Anthony, do you think?" she asked.

Money! That's where the old woman's thoughts were! Not with the little orphaned girl!

CHAPTER TWO

The nursery at 21 Eglinton Square was at the top of the house, and there Elizabeth lived with Bridie. The girl was not supposed to come downstairs. Mrs. Mercer wanted her out of the way. She couldn't believe that after all these years the care of a child was again her responsibility.

At dinner that evening, her husband told her something that unsettled her.

"The money is not all that much, Lydia. After our debts are settled, there's only twenty thousand pounds."

"Per annum?"

"No, in total!"

"That doesn't make sense, Anthony. Your Aunt left Frank a fortune. He cannot have gone through it all!"

"No, he did not. The balance, eighty thousand pounds, is left in trust for the child, to be hers when she attains majority at twenty-one years old."

Lydia put down her fork. Her appetite was quite gone.

"*Twenty-one!* That's preposterous! What was Frank thinking of? What an insult!"

Behind them, the footman, Forster, smiled inwardly. He was all ears. Young Mr. Frank knew his stepbrother and sister-in-law only too well it seemed. He slipped away and went downstairs. Bridie was there, relaxing for a little while, cradling the child in her arms, while Mrs. Chester, the cook was preparing the dessert for upstairs.

"She'll kill you for bringing the child down here," he remarked.

"Oh I don't care. Is the poor little one to be cut off from all human beings except me? She likes the kitchen, don't you, pet?"

Eliza nodded. Her calls for her mother had become less and less in the last few days. Bridie kept her occupied as best she could. She was very quiet.

Forster imparted the information he had heard to the rest of the staff. The upper servants were taking their tea in the housekeeper's room, so he could say whatever he wished.

"The greed of them!" hissed Bridie, cupping her hands gently over Elizabeth's ears. "Just think, this time last week, they were not expecting any money at all, then there's an accident, and they know that money's coming, and suddenly they can't live without a great big fortune!"

"The rich think differently than us," was Forster's reply. "Everything is about money. Where it comes from, where it goes, who has it, who hasn't. How long will you stick it out here, do you think?"

"Don't ask me that question. I want to see this little one settled and happy and then I'll be off."

"I think you'll be here for a long time, then." Forster smiled again. He liked the nursery maid.

"Go on with you," she said with spirit, seeing his look. "This is the worst nursery I was ever in. Old-fashioned and cold. Yes, cold! And this is July! We're going to freeze up there in winter even with a fire."

"Would she like a cup of warm milk?" asked Mrs. Chester. "And a little bit of this nice creamy meringue."

CHAPTER THREE

Eglinton Square had fine old houses, and most were very well kept. The Mercer house was good on the outside, but the inside needed redecoration. With Elizabeth's inheritance, the Mercers planned to renovate the house from top to bottom, with a few exceptions. The servant's quarters and the nursery were not on Mrs. Mercer's list.

The nursery had two interconnecting rooms which she had never expected would be used again. One was a bedchamber, the other a living room that had doubled as a class room and a sitting room.

"It's freezing!" Bridie was dressed in her warmest clothes even in October. She had a cold as did Elizabeth. The nursery fire was not lit until midday, and she was expected to make do with one scuttle of coal for the day. As she lived in the nursery with Elizabeth, this was not good at all for her health, and not good for the child.

"I'll have to speak to her about it tomorrow," she told Mrs. Chester when she was collecting the warm milk that evening. "It's so unfair. Even if they don't regard me, their child could get consumption!"

Accordingly she spoke to Mrs. Mercer the very next day.

"You're spoiled," her mistress remarked. "My former nursery maid never asked for favours."

"It's for Miss Elizabeth."

"My own children were very hardy. I did not spoil them."

Bridie was ready to walk out the door there and then, never to return, but the thought of Eliza at the mercy of that horrid woman was too much. She had to wait, but she felt she was coming to an impasse. Would the Mercers ever show affection to their niece? Mr. Mercer was morose. He reminded her of a bull with his broad shoulders and angry air, and she half-expected to see smoke coming out his nostrils. His wife had once been handsome, but a persistent feeling of the world using her in an ill way had spoiled her looks so that she now wore a perpetual scowl.

Mrs. Mercer went to the drawing room, made herself comfortable and opened a catalogue of furnishings from the best shops in London and Liverpool. Her husband arrived home soon after, and after they had dressed for dinner, she related how spoiled the maid was.

"Lydia, heed what she says! Did I tell you that if the child should not survive to twenty-one years, that her money is to be given to the church, to distribute to charities?"

"Your brother was indeed vindictive!"

"You had better order the fires lit earlier in the wintertime, and allow them to have more coal," he said tersely. He took up the newspaper then that was lying on the occasional table and browsed it for a few minutes before he started up. "Goodness, Lydia, did you see this?"

"I haven't read the newspaper," she said crossly. "I'm busy, I still have to decide between Turkish or Indian carpets."

"Why have we not heard about this? Our son's in-laws are selling their house and estate and moving to Jamaica!"

"Selling Sackhall?"

"Yes! And we have to have it, Lydia!" He got up, pacing the room. "There's a farm of course, and an army of servants and labourers. I'll be a Squire!"

Lydia began to envision herself the mistress of the great manor house with more servants than she could count at her beck and call. They could have hunting parties with the best people, why, Lady Fotheringale was a near neighbour, and there were other great gentlemen and ladies in the district. Her own origins were humble, but she had put them behind her and everyone associated with them. She'd married Anthony Mercer because the young mill-owner promised her the style of living that she aspired to.

"But what of this house?" she asked. "May we have two houses, Anthony?"

"The very thing, Lydia! This and our country estate! But they don't plan to vacate until mid-December."

"Our country estate! You must go tomorrow and make an offer. Millicent will be so proud to bring her children there on holidays, the country is healthy for children - oh dear."

"What is it?"

"Will we have to take - *her*? Her presence is very tiresome to me already."

"We could send her away to school."

"Why should we have the trouble of her education? She'll have holidays three times a year. I don't want her, and neither do you. Why did she not ...?"

"We'll have to place her somewhere until she's twenty-one," he said.

Forster appeared to say that dinner was ready, so they went in and said no more about the matter that evening.

CHAPTER FOUR

The Mercers realised after a short time and a lot of calculations that they could not afford two houses, so they put the Liverpool house up for sale.

Bridie was the first of the servants to know.

"We're not taking you with us," Mrs. Mercer said to her almost casually. "I shall release you from your work on Christmas Eve, with a good character reference and two weeks wages."

The prospect of a holiday at Christmastime was very appealing to Bridie. She could spend it with her mother and sisters and brothers. All of Christmas and New Year too! She had not done so since she was twelve years old and had to go into service as a junior nursery maid.

But what of Eliza? Mrs. Mercer though, was not as angry of late, and seemed to be more involved with the child, enquiring for her health and diet and supplying more heat. Perhaps she had simply needed time to get used to having a child in her life again. Bridie convinced herself that Elizabeth would be happier from now on.

Bridie was unaware that the reason Mrs. Mercer was easy and good-humoured was that she had decided where Eliza would spend her childhood, and it would be without any investment on their part at all. After their calculations they had realised that they would need every penny to run Sackhall's sprawling estate, and would even have to borrow. They then had had second thoughts about the expense, but were not going to back down and suffer the humiliation of telling their richer relations that they had misgivings about the purchase. They would find the money somewhere until the child came of age. (They never referred to her as Elizabeth) The papers were to be signed on December 22nd, and they would move on Christmas Eve.

She had something to attend to in the meantime. Donning a plain cloak and her oldest hat, she took a humble omnibus to Great Homer Street, to Paddy's Market, where she stopped at a stall with a mountain of children's clothing jumbled up on a table.

"What age is the little girl, ma'am?" asked the stall owner as Mrs. Mercer rummaged through the pile of little gowns, pinafores and shawls in a box, pulling them out and discarding them one by one.

"She's three."

"Oh aren't they darlin' when they're three! This is a beauty, ma'am. Hardly worn! Look!" The stall owner knew exactly where in the mountain to plunge her arm to find a little wool gown, red in colour, which she drew out and lifted up. "She'll love it on Christmas mornin', she will. It's in great condition, very warm. She'll be made up, she will."

"It's too good," said Mrs. Mercer, glancing at it and continuing to rummage.

"Too good!"

"Yes, I want something ragged."

"Somethin' ragged! Why would you want to put a child in rags, when you can do better?"

Mrs. Mercer had not thought about having to explain this. She was not a woman of imagination,

16

but a sign across the street caught her eye, "Dickens Emporium."

"It's for a play about street urchins. *A Christmas Carol.* I need very old, raggedy items."

"You've come to the wrong place, missus. I don't sell raggedy clothes to nobody. They goes out in the bin, they does." The seller seemed offended. She got tired of this customer thrashing around looking for rags in a pile of good, clean second-hand clothes, when there were two other customers she wished to attend to.

"You mean like what she's wearin'?" She indicated a little girl shivering on a nearby step. She was draped in a few thin rags. Her mother, equally attired, was selling some pathetic looking vegetables from a barrel.

"Yes, go and ask her for me." Mrs. Mercer rapped an order. She never had spoken to a beggar in her life.

"Why should I, when you're not buyin' from me? I 'ave real customers. Go an' ask 'er yousel'."

"I will buy her a set of clothes in exchange for those rags." Mrs. Mercer said sharply. "Now go and tell her."

The little girl got the red gown, which she was delighted with, and put it on straightaway. Mrs. Mercer went home with a parcel of dirty rags, which consisted of a tattered brownish dress with a threadbare petticoat, and a knitted shawl, frayed and threadbare.

CHAPTER FIVE

It was done, and they were free! On Christmas morning early, tomorrow, they would drive unencumbered to their new home. All their luggage had gone ahead of them. The servants had been sent out in advance to get everything ready for their ease and comfort, fires lit, a tree decorated, the aroma of Christmas dinner meeting them the moment they stepped in the door. The Princes had left all of their furniture, and though it wasn't to Mrs. Mercer's taste (dull and old-fashioned) it would do for the present.

"I'm glad that is taken care of," she said to her husband late on Christmas Eve.

"And very well, thanks to you," he said.

Early in the day she had told Bridie that she could go at seven o'clock that evening, and to save time, she would go to the kitchen and fetch the warm milk. As soon as she arrived in the nursery, Bridie would be free.

She had collected the milk from the cook, who wondered why the housemaid couldn't bring it, but she supposed that since it was Christmas, their mistress was making an effort.

Mrs. Mercer had stopped on the landing, and taking a little paper from her pocket, had shaken in some laudanum, about a quarter of what she dosed herself with.

"She's had her bath." Bridie said, smiling. "Here's your milk, Elizabeth, love."

The child was sitting up in bed and drank the milk. She lay down then and Bridie tucked her in.

"Are you packed? Leave now." Mrs. Mercer told Bridie. "I shall sit with her."

"Look, she's falling asleep already! The little eyelids are closing!"

"You will be able to take the last train home if you go now. Hurry."

"Thank you, Ma'am. Thank you. Bless you, and a Merry Christmas to you."

"And to you and yours, Bridie." She tried to hide her impatience.

Bridie bent to kiss the little forehead on the pillow, placed her rough hand on the fair head while she murmured a prayer, and left. Mrs. Mercer had gotten to work almost immediately. She would have to hurry! She retrieved the rags she had hidden in an old desk and dressed the now limp child in them. She'd debated about boots - no, they looked too fine. She'd have to be barefoot to resemble a poor child.

She then bundled her up in blankets and making sure none of the servants were about, brought her downstairs. Mr. Mercer drove the carriage to Vauxhall. She had heard that a group of nuns there looked after orphan girls, and were living in the house beside the church.

Anthony halted the carriage just around the corner from St Clement Square. He helped her out and with the bundle in her arms, she walked around the corner on foot. St. Clements church and convent buildings occupied most of one side of the Square, and she had hesitated before proceeding, but eventually convincing herself that she just looked like a mother or aunt carrying a sleeping child home after a visit to a friend or relative, she walked smartly on.

Then she had waited in the shadows of the high wall until she was sure nobody was looking, and she dumped the child on the convent steps, taking the good blanket away with her as she walked briskly away, up the side street where the carriage waited.

She had no fear that the girl would die of the cold for in just a few minutes the bells would peal out calling the faithful to Midnight Mass.

They were free! They had made their dream come true; an Estate of their own made them land owning gentry! They pushed from their minds the fact that it was ill-gotten.

CHAPTER SIX

Sister Clare smiled to herself as she made the manger ready for Christmas. It was placed just inside the side-altar and the statue of St. Rose of Lima had been carried away to make way for it. She was sure St. Rose didn't mind.

She thought the Nativity beautiful, for all its many years. The figures had been freshly painted, and a generous carpet of straw covered the floor of the wooden stable. The Virgin Mary wore a white dress and a long blue cloak bordered with gold stars, St Joseph was in dark green and brown and carried a lantern, the shepherds were in dark reds and greys. An angel in splendid gold leaf, a trumpet to her lips, adorned the top of the stable roof. It had been quite a job to place the angel in the exact spot she wished her to be, and there had been a little argument with the janitor, who disagreed, but eventually all were satisfied.

The manger itself was empty as of yet except for a lining of straw overlaid with a white lawn handkerchief. The Infant King would be lovingly carried up the central aisle of the church before Midnight Mass accompanied by 'Silent Night' from the choir, and placed in the manger.

"I love Christmas!" she whispered to Sister Anne, who was helping her finish the arrangement, placing holly boughs in strategic positions around the space.

"I prefer Easter," Sister Anne whispered back. "Christmas is very tiring. But you love little children, and little children love you. Push the donkey back a little bit. He looks as if he's going to eat the lamb."

"Like that?"

"Yes, and I never saw a cow that shade of red in my life; it's easily known you didn't grow up on a farm, Sister Clare!"

"How do you know what colour the cows are in the Holy Land, Sister Anne? I ran out of brown, and I needed to spare the black so I couldn't darken him.

Here, pull the straw up around him like that - her, I mean - and push her back to the back and now, look! She's in the shadow now!"

The two nuns were chuckling quietly at this when they heard the heavy doors open and clang shut again, and the sound of hurried footsteps approach. They looked around to see a man hurrying toward them, not pausing even to genuflect in front of the Blessed Sacrament.

"Sisters, there's a child on the convent doorstep," he said urgently, as he whipped his hat from his head and jerked his gloved finger to the doors. His greatcoat was covered in snowflakes. "She may be ill, or near death - she appears to be asleep, but when I bent down to gently shake her, she did not stir. She has neither cloak nor boots nor stockings. I saw the light and knew you'd be in here, so I thought I'd run and tell you rather than wait for someone to answer the doorbell -" he paused, breathless.

The sisters ran through the door that led directly from the nave of the church to the convent hallway. Within a few moments they had opened the large heavy door and shone the lamp outside. There, as the man said, lay a child on the step, her threadbare clothes draped about her like a thin mist, her head covered only by her long blonde hair. She was motionless, like a carved block of tinted ice, with blue lips and fingers and toes. She was either unconscious - or dead.

CHAPTER SEVEN

"Abandoned on Christmas Eve," Sister Anne sighed, as Sister Clare hurriedly carried the child into the warmth of the convent kitchen, set her on her lap by the large range and began to rub her hands. "She's alive, but very pale." She lifted one eyelid "Pupil dilated. Drugged? We had better send for the doctor."

"How do you know she is not lost?" asked Mother Maria, the nun in charge, approaching with an armful of blankets. She was an older woman from Turin in Italy.

"Look at the note pinned to her shawl, Mother."

AN ORPHAN

"Strange indeed! No name!" Mother Maria helped to wrap the child up in the blanket. "We must cover her head. She is more dead than alive! *Poverella!*"

"Who could have left her there?" sighed Clare.

"Her parents, perhaps, her desperate parents. Maybe from that slum down by the old market. Sister Clare, you will not be able to attend Midnight Mass. Better you go in the morning. What beautiful hair she has, golden! But be careful – they may have those – what do you call them …?"

"Now here's an odd thing, Mother Maria." Sister Clare exclaimed. "Except for her clothes, she's clean as a pin. Her hair has no sign of vermin. Her ears, clean. See her nails? Spotless! Her feet are not dirty. Freezing cold but not even a bit of grime on them, and soft, she doesn't go barefoot. She's also well-nourished!"

The two women looked at each other in astonishment.

"That is a mystery, Sister Clare! How many years has the poor *bambina*? Three?"

"About three. Too young to be able to give an account of herself even if she was awake," said Sister

Clare. "Sister Anne, see if you can catch Dr. Weldon before he goes into Mass."

Dr. Weldon came down to the kitchen ten minutes later. By then the little one was beginning to regain warmth in her feet and hands. She woke up and began to cry with the pain, heartrending shrieks as the blood coursed once again through numbed tissues. It brought tears to the eyes of everybody. It lasted about fifteen minutes, during which she did not seem conscious of where she was, did not call for anybody, though her dark eyes looked from Sister Clare to Dr. Weldon and back again. Her cries subsided and she fell asleep in Sister Clare's arms again, her thumb in her mouth.

Dr. Weldon too thought it puzzling that she had obviously being living in good circumstances. How did she come to be wearing rags like the poorest little urchin in the rookeries? It did not fit.

"It would be wise to let the police know," he said, "in case she was abducted. She may have parents desperately seeking her. She will recover."

A warm bed was prepared and she was tucked in and slept for the night.

CHAPTER EIGHT

Mr. and Mrs. Mercer arrived in their new home the following day, and had a wonderful Christmas, dining splendidly on roast goose, roast potatoes, partridge pie and all kinds of buttery and creamy side dishes. They drank a lot, rather more than usual, but would have denied that this was because they had something on their consciences. Their first day in their new house was perfect, and before the day was out, they were drawing up lists of prestigious people to invite to a Ball in the New Year. Thus they planned to introduce themselves to Society.

They gave no thought to Elizabeth except to remark that she was much better off with the nuns than with an indifferent aunt and uncle. Her twenty-first birthday was many years away. They had plenty of time to claim her before that, and to think up a plan that would bring her money their way as soon as she came of age.

When Mr. Mercer had too much to drink he became very morose. His aunt's betrayal of him many years before had caused him bitterness and he nursed this festering sore until it began to make him ill. His wife was equally bitter. They were supposed to be happy now, but somehow the events of the past six months had not made them so. It was supposed to have been their perfect Christmas but in the evening, the joy fizzled out, so Mr. Mercer drank a great deal of brandy and fell asleep on the sofa. His wife climbed to their bedroom alone, looking about her fearful of strange shadows. But she knew the shadows existed only in her mind.

CHAPTER NINE

On Boxing Day Sister Clare had a visit from her brother Eric, a Detective Inspector with the Liverpool Police. He brought his wife Dolly and his three children, Margaret, Lucy and Peter, a boy eight years old. Over tea and Christmas cake in the sedate parlour with the striped green and white wallpaper, she related the events of Christmas Eve.

Mrs. Reid often complained that her husband was never fully off duty, and she might have had cause to grumble today, for he asked so many questions, and probed so much, that it took up almost the entire visit. The engagement of her niece to a Naval Captain, which she had intended to be the main topic of conversation, faded into the background after an initial mention and short buzz of excitement.

Peter was sitting quietly on a straight-backed chair as he had been told to do, a plate with a slice of cake balanced on his knees. He swung his legs to and fro, rather dangerously rocking the china plate.

"Papa, will you check all the reports to see if there is a little girl missing?" he interposed with as much eagerness as his father.

"Here's another policeman in the making," Dolly said with amused resignation. "I think our son knows all Her Majesty's laws and bye-laws already."

"I'm going to be a Detective Inspector too," he announced.

"I'll be retired by then, or I'll be usurped by my own son," his father chortled. "Ah! Nuts in the Christmas cake! It's nothing without nuts, is it?"

"I like the cherries best," said Peter. "Lucy, if you don't like your cherries, you can give them to me."

"Peter!" exclaimed his mother. "Mind your manners – you're not at home now."

But Sister Clare laughed. "I love to see children being children, Dolly," she said. "But will you look into it,

Eric? All we can really get out of her is her name Elizabeth, and there's someone called Bridie she asks for."

"First thing tomorrow," he promised. "A child from a good home, dressed as an urchin, left on your doorstep."

"Papa, you have to see her for a proper description," Margaret interrupted.

Sister Clare disappeared and returned holding Eliza by the hand. She sat on Clare's lap and the nun fed her some cake.

"She's a little picture," Lucy said, smiling affectionately. "If I were writing her description, I would say 'golden hair,' and 'big brown eyes'.

Her father was too absorbed in trying to get words from the little girl.

"What's your name, pet?"

"Elithabeth Mary," she said.

"Ah, but don't you have a surname too?"

"Papa, she's too young to know what that is," Lucy said.

"Not at all. I made sure you all knew yours as soon as you knew your Christian names, in case you ever got lost."

"Elizabeth...?" He leaned toward her, his eyes bright and friendly. "Elizabeth...what comes next?"

Eliza's response was to make a face, remove a chewed up currant from her mouth and show it to Sister Clare. "I don't like that," she said.

"Oh, she's a darling!" sighed Margaret and Lucy, together.

"What's your Mamma's name?" asked Inspector Reid, in a very encouraging way.

"Mamma went away."

"But do you know your Mamma's name? Maybe we can find her, if you do."

"Don't upset the child," said Mrs. Reid.

"I'm not upsetting ..."

"Babth," said Eliza.

"Now, see?" said Mr. Reid with triumph. "Babs. Barbara."

Lucy got up from her chair and offered her a piece of Royal Icing.

"What's your Papa's name then?" asked Eric.

"I don't think you'll get any more out of the little one." Mrs. Reid said. "Oh, look at the time – we're expecting James and Sarah for tea –"

"Frank," said Eliza, taking the icing, as there was a loud rap at the door.

"Sister Anna's visitors," Sister Clare said quickly, getting up and setting Elizabeth on the floor.

"You're welcome," said Lucy to Elizabeth. "What a mannerly little girl!"

"His name is Frank, her father's name is Frank." said Peter. Nobody heard, for goodbyes were being said and several people were talking all at once.

"You will have to assign her a surname," said Inspector Reid.

"We had better go," said Mrs. Reid. "Next time, I'll tell you all about Gillian and Captain Westfall, he's so charming - dashing, in his uniform...Margret couldn't be more pleased...his great-uncle commanded..." she continued to talk about him as they went out the door.

CHAPTER TEN

"I think we're safe now," said Mrs. Mercer when nothing was reported in the newspapers about a little girl found on Christmas Eve.

"I was quite worried for a time, in case, but you did right to dress her in poor clothing, Lydia. Barefoot too! Nobody would ever guess she was from a good home."

"Anthony, we have to keep an eye on the child as she grows up. What if they send her away to the country or something, and we lost track of her?"

"How can we keep an eye on her, without revealing ourselves?"

"I have been thinking about it. Do you remember Miss Shields!"

"Our old governess? Miss Scowlface?"

"Yes, the very one. She would be very suitable. She's cunning, respectable, of good appearance, smooth and very pleasant when she wants to be. She can call on the convent, pretend some connection - that she it was who found her - and brought her there - and wants to know how she goes on, because she can't stop thinking about the unfortunate girl. She can make herself useful to the nuns."

"If she can make it plausible."

"She could also gain the child's trust, so that when she is sixteen or so, she will go to live with her, perhaps, and then - we'll have her!"

"A good scheme! Lydia, you are a genius."

"I don't think we need to let her know what our interest is in this child, Anthony. We can say she's a child we befriended. As for our never - or rarely - seeing her, that can be explained away. We'll have to promise her a good sum of money or something at the end of it, but make it clear that she is to get it only if she stays in our employ for all that time."

CHAPTER ELEVEN

The Refuge was a Girl's Home with only fourteen residents, and three nuns to look after them. A large plaque in the hallway stated:

JOY IS THE SIGN OF THE HEART THAT LOVES THE LORD

The Sisters were new in the city. They had begun by founding a club to give poor girls in the area something to do and to look forward to on Sundays. They gave them food and played games. After a short time, when it was evident that some of the girls were homeless, or lived in unbearable situations at their homes, they set up a Refuge. The girls were taught to read and write and St. Clement's Ladies Charity purchased sewing machines to train the girls in dressmaking. Above all, the girls were loved.

The Order had been founded to take care of girls older than Elizabeth but the nuns decided that since she had been placed on their doorstep on the very night that Jesus was born, that she was meant to stay with them. She was far too young for school so she spent most of her days with Sister Clare in the kitchen, playing with pots and pans and sticky dough that she shaped into the little animals that she saw in the garden. There was a spaniel, Tom, and the convent cat, Pippy. An occasional squirrel scampered up one of the trees, and if she was very quiet, she might see a rabbit near a wooden fence. In the spring crows built their nests high in the trees and sparrows under the eaves.

Her favourite place in the convent was the kitchen. Its door led to the outside and she wandered out at will. It was a very long garden with a vegetable patch, apple trees and flower garden with a wild section at the end overgrown with grasses and ferns which thrived in the shadow of four elms.

Sister Clare, who was the cook, was her constant companion. The nuns had chosen a surname for her.

They decided to give her a name in tune with the Christmas season, and chose Snowe. Elizabeth Mary Snowe.

"Sweet *bambina*," Mother Maria cooed whenever she visited the kitchen. "Come here to Mother!" She always threw her arms out wide and the little girl flew into them. Though they all loved Eliza, Mother Maria demonstrated affection with hugs and cuddles, and Eliza loved how she talked with her hands as well as her mouth.

Nothing further had been found out as to who she was. Nobody had reported a little girl missing. There were plenty of older girls who disappeared, many of them running away from bad homes or situations, often never to be seen again. Eliza had talked of somebody named Bridie for a little while, but by spring, had forgotten her and her other life. The nuns had concluded that Bridie was the maid who took care of her in the mysterious home where she had spent her earliest years. She was a quiet child.

CHAPTER TWELVE

Miss Shields knew the Mercers very well. She knew them to be unscrupulous, grasping people, and as she was cut from the same cloth, she understood them. She was the daughter of a textile baron who had lost everything when she had been nineteen years old. She had to support herself and loathed her life as a governess. But there was no other respectable way for her to maintain herself. She'd had an offer of marriage that she had declined, because he was too poor. Living by her own wits, she could do better.

"This commission we entrust you with, Miss Shields, is a very important one. You are to see the child frequently, befriend her, and take her to live with you in time. She is to grow up obedient, malleable and persuadable by those in authority over her."

"I would have thought the nuns would be good at that."

"Perhaps, but she must trust you, because there's something else. When she comes of age she is to be delivered to us. This is an extended commitment, Miss Shields, and we will recompense you handsomely. If you do your job well, you may expect, at the end of it, two thousand pounds, as well as your quarterly wages and living expenses for the next eighteen years of course."

The offer was irresistible. She had to accept. It promised stability. No more having to settle into a new family every few years, hating her small room, feeling the loneliness of a poor genteel woman who was neither servant nor family. She could live in one place and have the charge of one child only until she was grown and then retire.

CHAPTER THIRTEEN

Mother Maria went to the parlour to see the visitor. She found a tall, very neat woman who sat straight as a ramrod in her chair. She rose as Mother Maria entered, towering above her.

"Mother Maria," said the visitor, "I am a stranger to you, I know. Pray allow me to introduce myself. I am Miss Laura Langley. And when I tell you what I have done, and why I have come here, you may not wish to see me again, but I beg your understanding."

Mother Maria was very puzzled, but bade her visitor to be reseated.

"On Christmas Eve, I was walking home on Clement Street, and I saw a little urchin girl. She was alone, and looked so cold I took pity on her. I picked her up in my arms and brought her here, rang the doorbell and - this part I am ashamed of - I hurried away."

"I see," Mother Maria was considering her guest carefully. She was not sure whether to believe her or not.

"Did she say anything?"

"No, nothing at all. No doubt you think it strange that I did not wait to make sure she was safely inside, but I was afraid of being mistaken for her mother."

"You rang the doorbell? Nobody heard."

"I rang the doorbell," Miss Langley replied, for so Miss Shields had styled herself. "The reason for my visit today," she added hurriedly, "is because she's been on my mind constantly since then. I had to go away, but I decided that as soon as I returned I should call upon you and ask how she is. I regretted I did not wait, I have chided myself many times!"

"She goes on well, thank God. She was very cold and had been drugged."

"Drugged!"

"Yes, unconscious. But when you found her, she was awake then, yes?"

Miss Shields fumed to herself. Why hadn't the Mercers told her the entire story, that the girl had been drugged and unconscious?

"Yes, she was sitting on the ground, I asked her name. She then fell over, and I caught her up and brought her here."

"Did she tell you what her name was, Miss Langley?"

"Oh no. She made no answer. Pray, did she tell you?"

"It's Elizabeth," said Mother Maria, a little suspicious of this woman. "And I wish to tell you, Miss Langley, that there is an odd kind of mystery about her."

"A mystery!" Miss Langley's eyes widened and she sat even straighter.

"Yes, a mystery. The police are aware of our concerns." She watched Miss Langley keenly. But if she was perturbed, she did not show it.

"Mother Maria, I very much admire the work you do here in Liverpool. There is no greater service you can do for poor children than to get them in from the streets and into a comfortable home where they are fed and sheltered. I used to be a governess, and if you should need me to help in any way, I would be happy to volunteer my time and expertise to assist the girls in your care. That was my second reason for coming here today. I would like to lend a hand. This city has so many problems, and then there are the foreign sailors leaving girls in desperate circumstances - their children are abandoned - I have the necessary references of course." She had asked her friends to write a few made-up ones, for she was not known as Langley before.

Mother Maria warmed to her guest at last. It was not often that people offered help.

"Thank you. I will consider it. The older girls need some lessons in mathematics, simple mathematics to help them with their future living, and spelling and a good - *vocabulario* - are always helpful."

"*Italiana, Madre?*" Miss Langley smiled.

"*Si, si! Parli Italiano?*" Mother Maria's face lit up and Miss Langley knew that her doubts had left her. She answered in Italian and they had a lively conversation, Mother Maria ordered tea, and they spent a very pleasant half-hour conversing in Italian.

CHAPTER FOURTEEN

S o it was that 'Miss Langley' found her admission into the life at the convent. Though mostly occupied with the older girls, she soon found her way to the kitchen where little Elizabeth was. She used the pretext of looking for a glass of water.

"You didn't have to come yourself," Sister Anne said. Clare had had to go to the dentist, and Anne was preparing dinner, which they ate in the middle of the day. "You could have sent one of the girls."

"I am not accustomed to being waited upon," said Miss Langley. "What a nice bright kitchen you have here. And - is this Elizabeth?" She looked keenly at the little girl sitting on several cushions at the big table making shapes from dough. "My, she looks much better than when I saw her. She's put on weight; she was so thin, poor little thing! Just a skeleton!"

Sister Anne did not reply. Mother Maria had waxed too lyrical about this new teacher. Homesick for Italy, she'd been thrilled to find someone who knew her language. Anne, a very sensible woman, was skeptical.

"So you brought her here?" she asked abruptly.

"Yes, did Mother Maria not tell you?"

"Yes, she told us all."

"Do you know if Elizabeth has any family at all?" asked Sister Anne after a short pause.

"Oh no! How should I? Did Mother Maria not tell you I just found her on the street? I don't know anything about her background."

"I see," Sister Anne.

"Does Miss Elizabeth know her letters?" asked Miss Langley. "If not, I can teach her."

"She's too young yet."

"They cannot begin too soon to learn their ABC. I shall set some time aside daily to teach her," declared

Miss Langley, setting the empty glass on the table. "Elizabeth, would you like me to teach you ABC?"

"I don't know," was the response.

"I shall take that as a yes," was Miss Langley's response, "and we shall begin tomorrow!"

"I must check with Sister Clare first," said Sister Anne.

CHAPTER FIFTEEN

"There's something off about Miss Langley, Mother Maria." Sister Anne had requested a private word with the Reverend Mother and they spoke in her little office upstairs.

"She looks a bit severe, but she has good references," replied Mother Maria. "She's a caring woman. The world needs more women like Miss Langley."

"Then Mother, you believe her story about finding Elizabeth?" asked Anne. "For she told me that she was very thin, and we know she wasn't."

"I wondered about some things also, Anne," Mother Maria said. "But it would be very easy to make a mistake. She may have thought her to be an undersized child of six or seven."

"Pardon me, Mother Maria, but she did not look in the least surprised to find a very young child in the kitchen."

"Yes, well - it's all a mystery, is it not? We mustn't be suspicious of Miss Langley because she mistook her age. She will not take any pay, you know, for teaching."

"She wants to teach her the alphabet."

"Well, let her teach her! What harm is that? Now you must excuse me - I have to look at this bill from the coalman. He is to come tomorrow to be paid."

Sister Anne did not wish to disturb Sister Clare who was recovering from a painful tooth extraction, but the following day when she mentioned it, Clare was not troubled either.

"I have trust in Mother Maria's judgement," she said. "It wasn't good of Miss Langley to leave her there and run off, but perhaps she did take fright. I'm sure it will be all right."

CHAPTER SIXTEEN

Miss Langley rejected the lodgings the Mercers found for her, and was in a good position to demand better. After a time, she got tired of her job teaching the girls at the Refuge, and told Mother Maria that her health would not allow her to come three times a week, but she said she would come regularly to teach little Elizabeth. She was 'very fond' of the little girl!

The Mercers were under the impression that she spent most of her day at the convent with the child, but in reality she was visiting her friends and going to plays and amusements, on their money.

She wondered why they were very keen that Elizabeth be monitored. Only one reason made sense - she must be worth her weight in gold to them. She knew there had been a brother Frank, much younger and on a visit to Sackhall she asked Mrs. Mercer about his whereabouts.

"He drowned in a boating accident. I don't like to talk about it," was her reply, cutting off any further communication.

One day she found out the truth from the servant who brought her payment every quarter. Frank had been married, and they had a little girl! Now she knew who the child was.

'It must be her - and she's rich as Croesus, that girl. If the nuns find that out, they'll want her money for themselves! They'll try to get her to enter the convent for her money! I wonder what way it will all play out! I could always drop a hint to the Mercers that it may happen, and only I can prevent it!'

She only had one problem and that was Elizabeth herself. The little one was reserved with her. Even Miss Langley's years of teaching children did not provide her with the skills necessary to draw her out and gain her trust. At least Sister Anne, the suspicious one, was gone. She had been transferred to set up a new Refuge in Manchester. In her place was a quiet nun named Sister Grace who took no notice of her one way or the other.

CHAPTER SEVENTEEN

Sister Clare's mother was still alive. She lived with her son but due to ill health did not visit very often. She had met Elizabeth a few times and thought she was a very pleasant little girl. She also thought that her daughter was getting too attached to her. When she visited her in May, leaning heavily on her son Eric, she was determined to tell her so.

"What if you get transferred, Clare?"

"I will leave all that in God's hands," said Clare firmly. "Mother Maria has a very soft heart, like our Founder, Father Pacelli, God bless him."

"You might have done better to have married. You'd have children of your own. You're very motherly."

"I wouldn't be a good nun if I hadn't the qualities of a mother. My children are the unloved ones, the ones that find themselves thrust into a cruel and unfeeling world."

"You will have no shortage of children, then," observed her mother. She opened her reticule, taking out a little box.

"I want you to have this," she said, opening it and holding up a gold cross and chain. It had been a gift from Clare's father on their 25th Wedding Anniversary. "Will you be allowed to keep it, with your vow of poverty?"

Clare knew by the gesture that her mother thought she would not live much longer.

"Why don't you give it to Margaret or Lucy?" she said, trying to sound calm and normal.

"Mamma has given them many items of value." said Eric.

"That's true. I want you to have this. Will you accept it?"

"I shall ask Mother Maria, but I think it will be all right."

"And pray for me, Clare. My days are not long. Now none of that nonsense about living till I'm a hundred. I'm plain spoken. I have diabetes."

Clare hung her head. It was certainly hard to control her tears. She said an affectionate goodbye with her mother and brought the cross and chain to Mother Maria.

"It is an item of beauty, *si*, great beauty. I know its value to you is sentiment, not money. You may keep it."

"Thank you, Mother."

Two weeks later, old Mrs. Reid died, and Clare had occasion to appreciate having an object which had been a symbol of love between her mother and father. She wept in her little room, holding it to her breast.

Elizabeth came in then. She could never remember to knock, indeed, as the convent was her home, she roamed freely everywhere.

"Sister Clare! Why are you sad?"

"My mamma is gone to heaven, and I'm happy for her, but sad for myself."

Then Elizabeth said: "I think my mamma is in heaven too. Your mamma can say hallo to my mamma."

"What a dear you are! They can have a good chat!"

"And tea maybe!" Eliza put her little hand underneath the cross with reverence. She stared at the figure of Jesus on it.

"Why did Jesus die?"

"He died to take away our sins."

Elizabeth considered this.

"Will I be a nun, like you?" she asked.

Sister Clare's heart felt consoled. The innocence and pure heart of the child touched her.

"If that's what God wants you to do, then you will," she replied, her eyes shining with tears. "We are all sent into the world for a purpose, and you must pray to know what He wants."

"All right," said Elizabeth cheerfully. "Don't cry any more, Sister Clare. Your mamma and my mamma are eating marzipan in heaven." It was Eliza's favourite, of course! She departed, leaving Clare to smile through her tears and the memories of her mother.

CHAPTER EIGHTEEN

Elizabeth took her lessons in the upstairs classroom which looked out onto the garden. She was not really keen on academic subjects and was happiest downstairs in the garden, for she found plenty to do there.

In spring she looked for birds that had fallen out of their nests and if they were dead, she held little funerals for them. She and Tom were the chief mourners. He dug the holes with his front paws, and she placed them in, and then at her signal, he filled them in again. He loved his job a little too much perhaps, as occasionally he dug them up again and reburied them himself. The gardener Mr. Bolger related it all to Sister Clare. At first he had been annoyed at these antics in the garden, but even he was won over by Eliza's fascination for everything that had life, even worms.

"She 'as a way with animals. They love her. A regular St. Francis, she is."

Another reason that school was a trial was that Miss Langley's voice was bossy and hard, not soft and gentle like Sister Clare's.

One day when she was about eight years old, distracted from her lesson while Miss Langley was out of the room, Elizabeth got up and looked out the window and saw Pippy the cat prowl ever so slowly toward a little bird pecking at the grass. She immediately banged on the glass, frightening the bird away and causing Pippy to look up at the window with an expression of annoyance at being denied her prey.

"Why did you do that?" Miss Langley had just come back into the room and she snapped at her.

"I had to frighten away a bird, Pippy would have caught him and eaten him." explained Elizabeth with a gentle smile.

"So what? That's Nature! You had no business looking out the window during class time! Hold out your hand!"

"For what?"

"For punishment, that is what!" Miss Langley took a cane from the corner of the room. Elizabeth shrank away.

"I'll tell Sister Clare!" she cried.

Miss Langley put the cane away again. She chided herself for almost losing control. It must never happen again!

"I acted hastily, my dear Elizabeth. Here ..." she dug into her pockets and brought out a boiled sweet. "You did quite right. The cat is fed well enough and does not need to kill to eat. Now, read me your French verbs. When you grow up, you might become a governess, like me."

Elizabeth was silent, and applied herself. It took a week before Miss Langley felt that they were on friendly terms again, and she again mentioned that she could become a governess if she worked hard.

"I think I'll be a nun like Sister Clare," said Elizabeth immediately.

Miss Langley smiled. She could hardly hide her glee. The nuns had started on her already! What clever women they were, you couldn't be up to them. They'd found out who she was and where she came from! But she couldn't allow it to happen, of course!

CHAPTER NINETEEN

Christmas Eve was always special to Elizabeth. Sister Clare had told her that she had been brought to them that evening in a snowfall.

"I remember looking around and seeing people looking down at me, and I had a pain in my feet," she said. "Then somebody gave me a drink of milk and tucked me up in bed, like Bridie used to."

"Do you remember anything else about Bridie?"

"No, but there was someone else - someone I was frightened of, a woman and a man."

"Were they your mother and father?"

"Oh no, they weren't." She seemed quite decided about that and Sister Clare thought she was probably right.

"Is Christmas my birthday?" she asked one day.

"We don't know when your birthday is, Elizabeth," Sister Clare admitted. "You were about three when you came to us."

This made Eliza brood. Everybody knew their own birthday, and she had none!

"I have no birthday," she said sadly to Tom, the dog, patting his head. "I would like to have one. Do you have a birthday, Tom?" She was overheard by the gardener who reported it to Mother Maria.

"I do so wish there was a way to tell," Mother Maria lamented to Sister Grace. "It would have been so easy for whoever abandoned her to have written the date of birth down on the paper. Everybody is entitled to know their birthday!"

"They didn't care about her," Sister Clare replied sadly. "She could have been dead within an hour or fallen prey to some very evil people."

"I think we should have a special day to call her birthday," Sister Grace said brightly. "Allow her to choose a special Saint, and that Feast day can be called her birthday! Which saint does she like best, Clare?"

"Any saint who loves animals as she does. She especially likes to hear the story of St Jerome pulling the thorn from the lion's paw and how the lion became the pet of the monastery, but had his own job there, watching over the donkey, she makes me read it over and over."

"When is St. Jerome's Feast day?"

They looked up the Calendar of Feasts and found it was September 30th and decided to celebrate Elizabeth's birthday on that day. She told Miss Langley the next day she arrived.

"That's very nice," she said. *I'm sure I could find out when her real birthday is*, she thought to herself, *but there's no point.*

Out of idle curiousity, however, and with nothing to do one day, Miss Langley went to see the verger in the parish where Mr. Frank Mercer had been living. She asked to see the Register of Baptisms. She knew the year of her birth – '66 or '67. It did not take her long to find the entry, *Mercer, Elizabeth Mary, date of Baptism, March 2nd 1867.* As babies were often baptised the day after they were born, she thought that her birthday was the day before.

CHAPTER TWENTY

Sister Clare read stories to Eliza. She loved them and was learning to read so that she could read them herself. They opened up worlds to her that she never knew were there, worlds where children had mothers and fathers and when they grew up, married and had children of their own. Children had sisters and brothers and aunts and uncles and cousins.

"It upsets her a bit," Sister Clare confided in Mother Maria. "She wonders why she does not have all that, but she's too nice to say it outright, in case we think her ungrateful."

"Still, she must know what the normal world is about. That most children grow up in a family. And another concern is that she will need to know how to shop, and how to use money, and so on."

"I wonder if she shouldn't go out a bit, Mother Maria?"

"Yes, she should, but we cannot take her out. We can't go into public places like shops and amusement parks. What would the Bishop say? Miss Langley is the person to show her the world. I shall speak to her the next time she comes."

Miss Langley was very pleased to be granted the task. It would further the bond between her and Elizabeth. It surprised her that the nuns wanted her to see something of the world. What if she became attached to it and wanted to see more and more, and forgot that she was supposed to become a nun? Perhaps the nuns were not so clever after all.

She began to take Eliza out. Over the next few years they went out one day a month. They went shopping in the city, they walked along the docksides to see the great ships coming and going; they marvelled at Victoria Clock, and strolled in St. James' Gardens. They even went to an afternoon play at the Theatre Royal and a pantomime.

At one of these, Mr. and Mrs. Mercer arranged a 'chance' meeting. Miss Langley introduced them as the Harkness'. For their part they were very pleased with the healthy, pretty girl they saw. She was able to converse, though in a quiet and gentle tone, and her manners seemed submissive. In fact, she had taken an instant dislike to this couple, and she did not know why. She stood with her head lowered unless courtesy demanded she answer when she was spoken to.

They were very pleased with Miss Langley, still not knowing that she only visited the convent once or twice a month, and that all of Elizabeth's virtues, and most of her education, came from either nature or the nuns.

Unknown to the nuns who cared for her, Elizabeth often felt dejected. In her little room she wondered how she had come to be abandoned, and was sure that her mother and father did not care for her. All the children in books had mothers and fathers. The mothers and fathers cared for the children.

I'm different, she thought. *Why am I different?*

As she grew older, she saw more of the girls upstairs. One day she asked Helen, one of the older girls who had come to the Refuge. The ones who had been there when she had arrived were long gone, now as she grew, the new refugees were closer to her in age.

"We're all different in here," said Helen, threading her machine. "We've all had misfortunes. Some of us have no mothers, some of us have no fathers, some of us have bad mothers, some of us have bad fathers, some, like you, can't remember havin' any mother or father. We all 'ave a story. Mine is that my father remarried after my mother died and my stepmother didn't want me, so I lived homeless for a while and then I 'eard about this place so I came here. When I leave, I'll be able to set up as a seamstress."

"But I don't know who my parents are," Elizabeth said sadly. "I don't know where I'm from. I don't think my father and mother loved me. But Sister Clare says I'm to think of God as my father and Jesus' Mama as my mother and they love me."

"That's good enough, they do. Now I have to stop jabberin' or I'll never get this apron made up. Get your 'and away from the presser." The sewing machine began its work, the needle hopping up and down, making a row of straight stitches.

"I want to learn to sew like that," she said. "What's that wheel for?"

CHAPTER TWENTY-ONE

The Refuge expanded very rapidly, and soon they had taken in thirty girls and employed teachers for them.

"There's no reason to expect Miss Langley to keep coming in," Mother Maria observed. "She's given more than enough of her time already, and being part of a class will be good for Eliza. Perhaps Miss Langley would like to help out again with the older girls' education, if she wishes to keep coming."

But Miss Langley was not pleased. She saw her influence with Eliza diminish. She still had not gained the girl's trust and affection.

"Oh but I am so attached to her, please let me continue to see her," she pleaded, "I'm that fond of her, I look on her almost as my own niece."

Mother Maria's heart melted. It was very important for a child to have an adult in her life to look up to, someone out and about and in the world, not cloistered as she and the sisters were, and Miss Langley's words reassured her.

CHAPTER TWENTY-TWO

"**G**ood morning Father, have you come for your breakfast?" Eliza asked the priest shyly as he entered the convent hallway after celebrating early morning Mass. The sisters always gave him his breakfast in the small dining parlour where he ate alone.

"Yes, child. How are you today? Are your studies coming along well?" replied the black-cassocked priest. He smiled and placed his hand on her head to give her a blessing.

"There, you are all blessed for the day," he said, proceeding into his breakfast.

"Thank you, Father."

When Mother Maria came in, he mentioned that Elizabeth was growing up quickly.

"What are your plans for her?" he asked.

"She says she wants to join us when she is older," Mother Maria said.

"It's natural enough, when she's growing up here."

Father Collins dug into his boiled egg and toast. He had been up since five o'clock, prayed and celebrated Mass, and now it was getting on to ten.

"On the one hand, she will be used to convent life," said Mother Maria. "but on the other, how can she know about life outside, if she's grown up in here? Our ministry is to take young women from the streets. She is so sheltered from the world, I'm afraid she does not understand the difficulties many people face outside. She's also very *sensibile* – what is the word - sensitive. Perhaps that will pass, but she cried so many tears when we had to put Tom down. It was time, he could hardly move. Sister Clare had to cease reading her *Oliver Twist*. She feels others pains, even if they are people in books."

"Being out a bit more should open her eyes and be good for her."

"I would like for her to experience something of family life, and be part of all the – *alti e bassi* - ups and downs of peoples' days. Sister Clare's brother is a Police Inspector with a growing family. I haven't asked her yet, but I thought it might be a good thought if she went to them now and then. They are good Christian people."

"That would be a good experience for her." The priest buttered a slice of toast and agonised whether to put marmalade on it or not. He was praying and denying himself little luxuries for the conversion of a dying criminal. He resolutely set the knife down. "She has a different situation to the other children here."

"I will arrange it with Sister Clare."

"That will be good!" Father drained his teacup. "I must be off, and thank you for breakfast, as usual, it was excellent."

CHAPTER TWENTY-THREE

"**I**'m to go to Blackpool!" said Elizabeth with delight.

"Yes, my brother and sister-in-law want to bring you there with the family this year," Sister Clare was as happy as Elizabeth. She was moody lately, looking into space when she should be doing her little chores, and not paying attention to the person speaking to her.

"When am I to go? I can't wait!" she said, perfectly attending now. She was nervous as well as excited, she had never spent a night away from the convent.

At least she knew the Reids well. Frequent visitors to their Aunt Clare, she often went to the parlour to say hallo. Margaret and Lucy were several years her senior and made her feel special when they admired her hair or her ribbons. She received hand-me-downs from them, and she was happy to wear the gowns they had liked to wear when they were her age. She had never had anything new. Peter was always kind though he did not come as often as his mother and his sisters.

The day came at last and the Inspector called for her and walked her to their house, carrying her bag. She had never been there before and thought it small compared to the convent. But it was colourful and bright inside, and Mrs. Reid gave her milk and a bun before they set off for the station.

She had a moment of trepidation as she left for the train. She was leaving Liverpool! She almost panicked, but Margaret put an arm about her. "I want you to sit with me," she said, "because I want to show you everything as we go along."

She soon forgot her misgivings, and enjoyed her journey and later the first walk in Blackpool, along the pier. That night she slept very well after running and jumping on the beach and paddling in the water.

CHAPTER TWENTY-FOUR

It was time for Miss Langley's mid-year report to the Mercers, so she took a cab to their home. Mrs. Mercer was angry that the girl was gone to Blackpool.

"If she's getting away from us, if we lose track of her —"

"It's only for two weeks, Madam."

But Mrs. Mercer was very uneasy. A couple who took an orphan child on holidays with them could be thinking of adopting her. That would be ghastly.

"You've been seeing her now for many years, and you cannot see the danger here? She must regard *you* as family, not these Reids. And he's a Detective

Inspector, is he not? I shall not disclose this to Mr. Mercer."

Miss Langley wondered why.

"Why is this family interfering where they have no business?" she went on. "I've been paying you handsomely for many years now to be her friend and confidant so that at the proper time she can be delivered up to us. If anything goes wrong, I'll hold you responsible and you can repay all we've laid out on your ease and comfort, and there will be no lump sum."

"Harsh words, Madam!"

"You are to go to Blackpool immediately. I will leave it up to you to construct a scenario in which you take precedence over these Reids."

"If I'm to do that," said Miss Langley angrily, "I have to know more about this girl. All you have told me is that you're her guardians and you want nothing to do with her until she is twenty-one. She's an heiress, isn't she?"

Mrs. Mercer drew in her breath sharply. Miss Langley spoke again, rather angrily, her face betraying annoyance.

"If you tell me more about Elizabeth, about her early life before she went to the nuns, I'm in a much better position to do as you ask. You shouldn't be afraid of only the Reids. The girl, young as she is, wants to enter the convent! There! *All* her money will go to the nuns."

There was silence while this sank in.

"Very well then." Mrs. Mercer's tone was stiff. "The child is the daughter of my husband's wealthy brother Francis and his wife Barbara who were both drowned..." as she went on, Miss Langley was able to confirm that all she had gleaned from the servants years ago, was true. She was the minder of a very rich little girl.

CHAPTER TWENTY-FIVE

Miss Langley disembarked the train at Blackpool with one aim in mind, to find the Reid family and take the child away from them. Not completely of course, she had no intention of spending more time with Eliza than she absolutely had to.

She'd had an idea on the train. In Blackpool many years ago, she had her fortune told by a woman who styled herself *All-Seeing Ethel*, who owning a tent and a crystal ball, and cultivating an aura of mystery by wearing flowing garments, heavy jewellery and a red headdress, did a brisk business among tourists. Ethel's predictions of a 'tall dark stranger' had not come true, but money had come her way as she'd predicted, though Miss Langley thought that it was a lucky coincidence. She did not believe in supernatural powers, it was all a very cunning trick of telling people what they wished to hear, by subtle but leading questions and keen observation.

She made her way to the fairgrounds hoping that the tent was still there, and it was. Once inside, instead of consulting her about her own fortune, she explained herself as plausibly as she could.

"The little girl desperately wishes to know where she comes from. I want to make her happy. There are certain things I want you to tell her, to put her mind at ease."

All-Seeing Ethel looked doubtful. "I don't know about that. What if I see different?"

Miss Langley suppressed a laugh. "Allow me to explain more. She has to get the impression that they live very far from here, and that she must keep it secret, or there will be bad luck. And – that she's to look to me to guide her in everything, because she's a remarkably foolish girl, Madam Ethel, and impressionable. I know what's best for her."

"How old is this child?"

"She is nine years old."

"Too young. I can get into trouble, you know. I keep one step ahead of the police. Any excuse, they run us off."

"I'll pay, Madam Ethel. Four shillings."

"All right then, but don't expect me to frighten a child, understood?"

"Oh no, my intention is not to frighten her. Now this is what I want you to say..."

CHAPTER TWENTY-SIX

The Inspector had to return to duty after three days of holiday, but left his wife and family in Blackpool. Peter missed him. He was stuck with all these women! He got bored of being around them all the time and decided to go for a stroll around the shops, his holiday money jingling impatiently in his pocket, to see if he could buy a kite.

"Do not go into the Fairgrounds," said his mother sternly. "We will go there later in the week, all of us together. I don't want any of my children alone in a place like that, full of odd people."

Peter did not mind - his money was for a kite.

He knew Blackpool and stopped to look at the Tower, wondering if anybody had attempted to climb up the outside, and deciding that his mother would have something to say if he was seen attempting it. He went on, whistling, and found himself passing the Fairgrounds. There were many people there, for the amusements were open. He was not about to go in of course.

As he went by, he spied a large tent, and would have thought nothing of it if he did not see the figure coming out. It was a tall woman, rather severe looking, and he knew she was from Liverpool, but could not place where he had seen her before. What did it matter? Half Liverpool was here and his father said that the other half were from Manchester. But his young mind filed it away. Imagine anybody being stupid enough to visit somebody who claimed they could tell the future! And there, as she came out, another woman went in. What a waste of their money!

He did not get a kite - he did not see any he liked enough to buy, so he went back to the boarding house later for his tea. His sisters were chattering madly about some young men they had seen. His mother was reading a book, and Eliza had a top. She was trying to get it to spin without much success, so he helped her and showed her exactly how it should be done. He had more strength and made it spin very fast and for a longer time, and she smiled brightly as she watched it go around.

There was a knock on the door, and then the landlady showed a woman in - the tall woman he had seen earlier visiting the fortune teller.

"Miss Langley!" said Elizabeth immediately, with amazement but with little pleasure. If anything, Peter thought her face fell.

So that's who she was! He had seen her a few times when he'd run an errand for his mother to the convent. Miss Langley, the woman who visited Elizabeth and taught her things and took her out.

His mother had met her before also, and rose to greet her. She sat with them for a while, explaining that she too had planned to come to Blackpool this week, and when she'd seen them earlier, she found out where they were staying and decided to pay them a call.

Elizabeth continued to spin her top though with less enthusiasm than before. He noticed that Miss Langley kept looking toward her, smiling, as if to catch her eye.

"While I am here in Blackpool, would you mind if I took Miss Eliza out tomorrow afternoon? I saw a shop with some very nice materials in it, and one of them has colour I know she likes. I would like to get it made up into a new gown for her. You like turquoise, do you not, Elizabeth?"

She looked up and said "Yes, Miss Langley."

"I'm sure that will be all right," said Mrs. Reid.

"It will just be for an hour or so, then I shall deliver her back to you."

"That's settled then. Two o'clock tomorrow." Miss Langley rose.

"Goodbye, Elizabeth."

"Goodbye, Miss Langley," was the formal answer.

Peter thought that Eliza did not like Miss Langley, and come to think of it, neither did he.

CHAPTER TWENTY-SEVEN

"Now, before we go to the shop, Eliza, I want to take you to see an old friend of mine. She's going to tell you some very interesting things."

"What things, Miss Langley?"

"I know the dearest wish of your heart - it's to know who your mamma and papa are, and where they are. Is it not?"

Elizabeth's heart skipped a beat.

"Yes, it is. I wish I knew why I have no mother and father! I wish it every day!"

"Depend upon it, you do. This lady I'm taking you to, you must not mind that she looks a little strange - she dresses oddly, and wears carmine on her lips and has a red headdress, and she works in a tent. She has a crystal ball on a table - such a sight to behold, all sparkles and light! She has special powers and can look into the ball and tell you things."

"Special powers? You mean - like the saints had?"

"Sort of like that."

"The saints had no powers of their own; it all came from Jesus. Do her powers come from Jesus too?"

The words stuck in Miss Langley's throat. Not believing that Ethel had any special powers, she had to make Elizabeth believe that she had.

"She never said where they come from. But where else could they come from?"

"The Devil." Elizabeth immediately said.

"Who told you that? There is no such person, you know."

"There is, he's a bad angel and tempts people to do wicked things."

"Mrs. Ethel has powers, but they do not come from the Devil," said Miss Langley. "And – this must be a very great secret. Just between you and me. Do you understand? You cannot tell Sister Clare, or Mother Maria, or Mrs. Reid, or Miss Reid, or anybody at all."

CHAPTER TWENTY-EIGHT

Blackpool was packed. Families came in the hundreds week after week and the wealthier people brought their servants.

The Whyte family had three children and Bridie Ryan had had a very busy day. Thankfully, the children had worn themselves out running up and down the beach and fell soundly asleep at eight o'clock.

She herself fell asleep shortly afterwards and had a strange dream. It was about Elizabeth Mercer.

Elizabeth was in danger - some danger she could not put a name on. There were people – more like shadows – on the dark side of a curtain beckoning to her. One woman held a crystal ball, and smiled and beckoned. Eliza was unsure what to do.

She woke up suddenly and got out of bed. She gazed out the window at the moon making silver ripples on the sea. The dream had been so vivid that it had shaken her a little.

She had not heard anything of Eliza in the years since she had left the Mercer's employ. She hoped she was happy – but was she? In looking back, Bridie knew she had convinced herself that Mrs. Mercer had changed, grown warmer and softer, and would love the little orphan girl. Did she?

She had a photo of Eliza with her parents, and one of herself with Eliza too, taken just a few weeks before her parents drowned. She treasured them. The couple were so lovely to work for, young, in love and devoted to each other and to their little girl! She'd never since found a family as nice as they. She wondered if Eliza had any memories of them.

Now she felt a strong urge to pray for Eliza, wherever she was. She knelt by her bed and made the Sign of the Cross and began. She prayed the protection of Jesus on her.

CHAPTER TWENTY-NINE

"**P**eter, you have had a funny look on your face nearly all day," said Mrs. Reid to Peter. "What is the matter?"

"It's that Miss Langley," said Peter slowly. "I don't like her, and neither does Eliza."

"I noticed that too," said Margaret. "Even when she was promised a new dress, she didn't smile."

"So you're uneasy that she took her out? She does that all the time in Liverpool. What harm can she come to? The nuns trust her."

"I saw her coming out of a fortune-teller's tent yesterday," said Peter. "I passed the Fairground - just passed it Mamma, I didn't go in - and I saw her coming out of *All-Seeing Ethel*.

His mother was surprised, but silent.

"Foolish woman to waste her money like that," she said in a dismissive way.

"Oh, a fortune teller!" said Lucy. "She might tell me about who I'll marry! May I visit her, Mamma, when we go to the Fair?"

"You will do no such thing," her mother said, "Come along, it's a beautiful day, and we're wasting it. Come with us, Peter."

Peter went rather reluctantly. But he changed his mind and went uptown instead of the beach. Something was off. He turned his steps toward the Fairgrounds.

I knew it, he said to himself after a short, brisk walk. Ahead of him was Miss Langley and Elizabeth. He did not know what to do, and wished his father was with him. He knew that fortune telling, while not exactly illegal, was not really a crime either, unless there was a victim - someone who had been promised something and been defrauded. His father had no time for con artists.

The woman and child turned in the Fairground gate, and Miss Langley opened her reticule and took out the admission fee. *Perhaps they're not going to the fortune teller, perhaps she's taking her for a ride on the merry-go-round, and I'm a suspicious person to think she's up to something.*

But they were walking now in the direction of the tent. What to do now? What would his father do? But his father had his policeman's badge! He was just a boy.

As they stopped and took their places in the queue, Elizabeth spotted him and waved, a big smile on her face.

He saw Miss Langley stare at him, and he saw in her glare the hostility and evil-mindedness in her heart. Did it concern Eliza? He liked the little girl.

Miss Langley did not leave the queue, and when it was their turn, they went in the tent flap. Peter walked up to the gate, paid the sixpenny fee, and he too was inside the Fairgrounds. He sauntered about, taking a wide turn to end up at the back of the tent. There was nobody there. He lifted up the bottom edge, and crawled a little under it, flat on the grass with his head inside, his body outside. He was just behind the chair of Ethel. Her long scented robes were spread out on either side. Her feet were under a voluminous tablecloth that draped the floor. He could not go any farther without the risk of being detected, so he remained as still as he could.

Outside the tent, at the front, two women had seen the child being taken into the fortune-teller.

"That should be illegal," said one indignantly. "An impressionable child!"

"I had a funny dream last night about a fortune-teller," said the other, "and a little girl I used to be nursemaid to. Elizabeth Mercer."

"Bridie, I'm coming out in goose pimples, so I am. Would that be 'er?"

"No, that child is poorer than Miss Elizabeth. And that's not the Aunt. Whoever it is, she shouldn't have brought a child to a fortune-teller. Look at the time - I have to get back by four or Mrs. Whyte will have a fit. Two hours of looking after her own children and she's fit to be tied. Come on, Molly."

CHAPTER THIRTY

Peter was very still. Nobody had noticed him, at least not yet.

"Are you going to tell me who my mother and father are?" Peter heard Eliza, who was most likely seated at the other side of the table, eagerly ask.

"It depends, my dear, on you. You have to make promises."

"What are they?"

"That you must always regard Miss Langley here as your *dearest* friend, for she has your interests at heart, and you *must* obey her in *every* way."

There was only a little pause before Eliza said, "All right!"

"And you must never tell anybody about your parents, and how you found out about them."

"Why can't I tell people about them?" Eliza sounded bewildered.

"Because it will bring you bad luck."

"Do you know my real birthday?" asked Eliza, eagerness in her voice again.

"If you promise everything, I shall tell you everything I see here in this here ball. But you must promise. And - if you break your promises, you will have the worse luck all your life. I don't mean to frighten you, but that's the rule of the Unseen World."

"You might even die." said Miss Langley with a slow, dramatic air.

Penny Dreadfuls were not as bad as this, Peter thought. He'd been often tempted to read them, but his father banned them. His friends described lurid tales and gruesome murders.

"I promise," said Eliza.

Oh you silly little girl, Peter groaned to himself. He wished to intervene, but was afraid to. He wished he was older and had authority. He was afraid of Miss Langley.

"Good girl, you shall not regret it. There will be great happiness in store for you. Now I shall tell you what I see here..." Peter saw two fat arms raised up and descend again. A sudden heavy scent hit his nostrils making him want to sneeze. He stopped himself by pushing his nose into the ground.

"You were born on March 1st, 1867."

"Oh my dear, your real birthday is in March!" he heard Miss Langley say.

"Your father is a blacksmith in Scotland. Your mother is his wife." There was silence. "They are good people, though poor. Remember, you are not to tell anybody."

There was silence.

"Is that all?" asked Eliza, obviously disappointed, and hoping for more. "Isn't there anything else? Do I have brothers and sisters?"

"No."

"Why did my father and mother not want me?" her voice was very low and sad.

"They were very poor, I expect," Miss Langley put in.

"Very poor!"

Ethel peered into the Ball again. "They were poor, wretched poor. So they brought you to Liverpool and left you there. They knew somebody would rescue you. And Miss Langley here, along she came, and brought you up."

"I brought you to the nuns, Madam Ethel means." Miss Langley put in.

"What about Bridie?" the question from the little girl was unexpected and Ethel was not prepared. She peered into the ball.

"Bridie – is your mother's name."

"No, that was Babs," was the reply, very definite.

"It's the same name, really," said Miss Langley.

"Is it?"

"Yes."

"But - Sister Clare told me that I was not a poor child, that they only dressed me in rags. I was clean as a pin, and my hair smelled of roses."

There was silence in the tent, but Ethel was skilled.

"Why, of course, here it is - now I see it - your mother bathed you in rosewater, but your clothes had been stolen, so all she had to put you in was a few old rags."

Don't believe that rubbish, Peter said silently to Eliza. He was feeling uncomfortable and cramped, and as his body was sticking out, feared that someone would come by and raise the alarm.

"What's my surname?" asked Eliza.

"Why, did we not say? It's - Stuart, yes, Stuart."

"How do you spell it?"

"Spell?"

"S-t-u-a-r-t most likely," prompted Miss Langley. "Is that it, Madam Ethel?"

"Yes, indeed so, exactly as you say, Miss Langley."

"What was my father's Christian name?" asked Eliza.

"Hamish."

"There, now you have the details," said Miss Langley. "We will leave now."

"But I want to know more!" cried Eliza. "Where in Scotland do my parents live? I want to write to them!"

"Oh my dear! The ball is dull now, there is no more to be discovered. That will be five shillings, Miss Langley."

An argument ensued and Peter wriggled himself backward out of the tent and sat on the grass for a few minutes. His heart boiled over with indignation. How dare they! None of that was true! He remembered something - the Christmas a long time ago when she had said her father's name and nobody heard but him. What was it? He could not remember.

He ought to go and find a policeman to investigate this Ethel - and Miss Langley too but he had disobeyed his mother and he did not want it to get to her ears.

CHAPTER THIRTY-ONE

Peter continued his search for a kite and found one that he liked this time and bought it. The strange episode temporarily forgotten, he ran to the beach to fly it. His mother and sisters had gone back to the house. Good! He could have it to himself without Lucy demanding he share it with her before he had had a good run with it! He unwound it with excitement and then was joined by a few other boys flying their kites and they had an enjoyable time before Margaret was sent to look for him to tell him that the tea was ready.

His bothersome thoughts about the afternoon's happenings recurred. He knew he could not tell his mother he was at the Fairgrounds, because she would report it to his father, and the whipping he'd be sure to get would hang over him for the remainder of the holiday. But he and Margaret were close, so on the way up to the boarding house, he told her all about it.

She was very annoyed, but not with him. She was angry with Miss Langley and the woman named Ethel. When they returned Elizabeth was sitting at the table, and she was very quiet and sad, prompting their mother to ask her if she did not like Blackpool?

"I like it very well, Ma'am."

"But you are not happy, child? Are you ill?"

"No, Ma'am."

"Perhaps she walked too much in the sun," said Margaret. "She's tired, that's what."

"That may be it; you may go to bed directly after supper, Eliza."

Eliza climbed the stairs a little later and made herself ready for bed. She said her night prayers before getting in and lay her weary head on the pillow, wide awake.

She wished she had not found out who her parents were. It was better to remember them as misty shadows that could have been anything and that she was stolen from them. Mrs. Reid came in to tuck her in, and felt her forehead, and told her that she would feel fine in the morning. She felt better for the attention.

She awoke the following morning to the sun streaming in the window, and resolved to try to enjoy the day. Sister Clare had often told her how to do it. It was to start thanking God for everything you had instead of 'dwelling in misery', as she put it.

But this time, it hardly worked. After breakfast Margaret called her to walk outside with her for a little while, and Peter joined them.

"We know where you were taken yesterday, Eliza. And what you were told."

"How?" she was all amazement.

Peter told her he had listened in.

"You're not to believe that woman," Margaret said to her, putting an arm about her shoulders. "She has no powers and guesses everything and makes things up. She doesn't know who your parents are. She tells people things for money."

A load rolled off Eliza's soul.

"She fooled Miss Langley too!" she exclaimed.

"It's not for me to say anything about Miss Langley; but she should have had more sense."

"She paid her five shillings!"

Margaret was astonished beyond words. How could the woman be as foolish as that? It was very odd indeed!

"She told me that I had to obey Miss Langley, and should I?"

"Miss Langley is trusted by the nuns, so I suppose you should."

"I'm glad my parents didn't bring me all the way from Scotland to Liverpool. It would have been a long, long way."

"I'm sure there are plenty of nice places in Scotland where they could have left you," said Peter kindly. "Did you see my new kite? You can have a turn at flying it, if you like."

Eliza beamed. As Peter watched the little girl run and jump in delight, he was glad she seemed to have forgotten her sorrows. What happened to her yesterday wasn't fair.

When he got to be a policeman, he'd conduct an investigation and find out who her parents were and give her their real names.

CHAPTER THIRTY-TWO

Miss Langley decided to go and tell Mrs. Mercer of her personal success.

"I must congratulate you, Miss Langley," said that lady, after she had given her account. "You really are very clever. I never would have thought of it. And she's to obey you, or something bad will happen to her. Excellent."

"Thank you, Madam, but I have a little problem I must tell you about, that is, life in the city is getting more expensive by the day, and my lodgings have gone down – I found mouse droppings in the hall the other day, I was disgusted. You know how obsessed I am with cleanliness. There is a suite of rooms in Pruitt Place, very nice, and it comes with two servants."

Mrs. Mercer pursed her lips.

"You ask me for far too much," she said.

"The nuns are working on her, Madam, they must have got wind of something."

Mrs. Mercer took a sharp breath.

"She must not enter the convent."

"Then I will have to take her more and more away from it to get her used to the world. You said that she was to come and live with me, did you not? I shall have to have good apartments to take her to, to train her in the ways of a lady."

"I'm in no position to refuse you."

"Thank you, Madam!"

"Another matter, Miss Shields. There is something else you will have to guard against. In a few years, she will shed her childhood. She is not to meet any young men who will turn her head. She will marry, but not before she's twenty-one. We will choose her husband."

"I will see to it, Madam, that she will not meet anybody. And I know I can depend on the nuns not to allow her any consorting."

That evening, a germ of an idea came to Miss Langley's mind. She entertained and expanded it, smiling to herself. It was only a dream really, she could not pull it off - no - it was too daring - but when Eliza turned twenty-one, why should she turn her fortune over to the relations she never knew, when she'd known her, Miss Langley, all her life?

Why indeed!

CHAPTER THIRTY-THREE

1

882

"Are you sure you want to be a policeman?" Mrs. Reid groaned. "The hours, the pay, the danger from criminals, the beat in all weathers - I'd much prefer to see you in an office or a factory."

"Oh Mother how I would hate to be cooped up all day!" Peter wolfed down a ham sandwich. "No, a policeman I will be. A detective. Are we going to see Auntie Clare on Christmas Day?"

"Yes."

"Will Elizabeth be there?"

"I suppose she will, what is it to you?"

"I - I like her, that's all. But don't worry, Mother, she's too young for me. She's only fifteen."

"Don't marry until you're thirty, Peter. And another thing - I don't want you to get your hopes up - Eliza wants to be a nun."

"Oh." Peter put down his sandwich. His mother saw his face fall.

"You mustn't interfere with God's call, if He calls her to His service," she said quietly,

"Of course not," Peter said in a low tone. His mother could see his disappointment. She did not want him to get entangled when there was no hope.

On Christmas Eve, Elizabeth was in the church arranging the Nativity figures. Sister Clare was busy in the sacristy. The nuns' ministry had grown and expanded in the last few years, they now had forty young women and girls to care for. Eliza was among the eldest and helped with the younger ones. The organist came in and began practising his carols, the gentle strains of 'See Amid the Winter's Snow' and 'Silent Night' filling the dimly-lit church.

I love Christmas, she thought, though she could never forget that she was abandoned that day many years ago, she was now trying to be positive about it, and look at it another way. She was found. She could not be a sad nun. Sister Clare was concerned that she was melancholic sometimes, but Sister Clare did not know that the reason for that melancholia was that she had to spend time with Miss Langley, who she still feared. She obeyed Miss Langley because of fear, and never told her anything she felt she might disapprove of.

JOY IS THE SIGN OF THE HEART THAT LOVES THE LORD

She saw the plaque in the hall nearly every day of her life. She tried to be joyful. But something in her heart was dried up. She could not explain it to anybody, except maybe Peter, her best friend. Eliza told herself that she was not interested in him as a suitor.

Of late, though, she had feelings that worried her a little. She began to feel attracted to him, to almost long for him to draw nearer to her, rather than keep a little distance as was proper. His face, which she had never thought about as handsome or not, had attained a very agreeable look, especially with his neat handlebar moustache, waxed just a little, and his clear, grey-blue eyes. She looked forward to him coming to the convent and after he had left could not stop thinking of him. And he looked splendid in his police uniform! She fled from those feelings and was annoyed with herself. She was going to be a nun! It was all arranged, even if the nuns themselves weren't sure about her.

She went to a pew and said the prayer that was close to her heart, the one that Sister Clare had instructed her to pray over and over:

"Lord, show me Your ways, teach me Your paths, be it done unto me according to Your will."

Peter was working Christmas, but he saw Eliza early in the New Year when she visited his home. Her manner toward him was very friendly - almost coquettish at times - and he wondered if his mother's information was correct. It would not do to try to engage her affections; she was too young, and he was only a poorly paid young constable.

He remembered the resolve that he had at thirteen, that when he was a policeman he would attempt to find her parents, both to be helpful to her and to expose Miss Langley, for he liked her no better and when they accidentally met she was very wary of him and he of her. But he was very busy and his days were long and very full. Time off for a recruit was very sparse.

One day Eliza met him unexpectedly on his beat - she had just happened to take this street - she said, blushing - and he knew it was not true - he decided to bring up the delicate subject. She listened, a finger on her chin.

"I would like to try, when I have the opportunity," he said. But a shadow fell over her face.

"I don't know, Peter. Maybe I'm better off not knowing. My feelings are so up and down about it. I don't believe a word of what that fortune-teller said. You and Margaret were very kind to me that time in Blackpool."

"How could we have been otherwise?"

She looked up and smiled, a smile that warmed his heart.

"There's one thing you should know," he said slowly. "I should have told you. Do you remember what your father's name is?"

"No, I never did remember."

"I think you did, Eliza. The first time we met, it was in the convent parlour that very Christmas, and my father asked you, and you said it. But everybody was talking together, my father didn't hear, and Margaret thought you were saying something else - I tried to get them to listen, but they wouldn't listen. And now - I've forgotten what it is too."

"Oh."

"Sorry," he said. "I was just a child of eight. I remembered for a while and then forgot. But I do remember that you said it."

When he went home that evening, he had his supper and later took a stroll to Margaret's house with Lucy. Margaret had married and lived only a few streets away.

"Do you remember the first time we met Eliza?" he asked them over a cup of tea and biscuits.

"Oh yes, the parlour on Boxing Day."

"Papa asked her what her mother's name was, and she said 'Babs'."

His sisters nodded.

"Then, he asked her what her father's name was."

"Yes, I think I remember that," Margaret said.

"She answered."

"No, I don't think she did."

"What I remember," said Lucy, laughing, "was that she took a chewed currant out of her mouth and showed it to Aunt Clare, and said she didn't like it! And then you gave her a piece of Royal Icing, Mags."

"So I did! She said 'Thank' just 'Thank', very prettily."

Peter's brow was furrowed in a deep frown.

"Wait - no - she didn't thank you."

"Oh, she did too. She said *'Thank.'*"

"No, Mags! She said 'Frank'. I heard it clearly - she was answering Papa. And I tried to get you all to pay attention, but we were all going out the door because there were visitors coming in! Nobody listened to me."

"Is that it? Frank is her father's name then? Francis!" Lucy exclaimed.

"So that's Babs - or Bridie - and Francis." Peter said.

"No, Bridie was somebody else." Margaret stated.

"Are you sure? I had the impression they were one and the same person."

"Babs is Barbara. Bridie is Bridget. Aunt Clare thought she must be a maid. An Irish maid."

"Are you going to make enquiries?" Lucy asked with eagerness.

"I don't know." He looked a bit disappointed. "She's not sure if she wants to know, now. She said she's all 'up and down about it'. I suppose I'll leave it."

CHAPTER THIRTY-FOUR

Eliza did not like going to Miss Langley's apartments and felt guilty about not feeling more attached to the woman who was evidently devoted to her. But she had to admit that Miss Langley's apartment was comfortable, more so than the convent, with carpets, long velvet drapery, blazing fires in winter and superior food. Eliza had her own room there.

Miss Langley introduced her to her friends as her 'niece' which surprised her. Eliza was reserved among her friends, who were an odd assortment of older people. None of them seemed to be churchgoers and their conversation was worldly and usually about money and how to get more of it. They also tended to ridicule people who believed in a Power greater than they. This greatly surprised Eliza.

Among Miss Langley's friends was a man of middle age named Mr. Heppleworth. He was kind to Eliza, and she felt that of all Miss Langley's friends, he was the only one who tried to draw her out and see what interested her. She told him of her love for animals and how she wished to join the Royal Society for the Prevention of Cruelty to Animals. She even told him the story of St. Jerome and the lion, which he said he would try to believe, but in his view no lion ever made friends with a human being. And what did they feed him on, he asked then, laughing a little.

Mother Maria was under the impression that Miss Langley was a devout Christian. But there was no sign of anything in her home that said she was Catholic, or Protestant, or any other faith, no Bible, holy picture or anything else.

One day in October she settled into her room as usual and was surprised to hear a man's voice come into the sitting-room. When she came out, she was introduced to Mr. Shields, an attorney-at-law and cousin of her patron.

"My cousin wishes to adopt you, Miss Snowe," he said. Miss Langley smiled that bright smile that always unnerved her a little.

"I'm going to be a nun," she said with defiance.

"I am sorry to disappoint you, dear, but no, you are not, for they don't think you suitable for the life." Miss Langley said. Eliza was surprised that it had been discussed. Mother Maria should not have done that. "Mother Maria tasked me with breaking the news to you," she went on.

Eliza thought that was unkind of Mother Maria and showed how duped she must be by Miss Langley. She sat down and clasped her hands, but strangely did not feel very disappointed. An image rose before her eyes - that of a tall police constable, with a handlebar moustache and eyes that looked on her with affection.

"I can't be adopted unless my mother and father are dead, and I don't know if they are." Eliza said then, coming back to the point.

"They are most likely dead," said Miss Langley. Eliza looked at her curiously.

"Why do you think that?" she asked.

"Because they were poor crofter folk, and they have hard lives, and there are many orphans your age in Scotland."

"Scotland!" Eliza tossed her head. "I never believed that silly story. Why do you want to adopt me?"

"I have no family, and you have no family, so I thought we could make one family, you and me. But it doesn't matter. If you are not so inclined I don't mind so much as long as we are friends and can spend time together as we have always done."

"Of course, Miss Langley." Eliza managed a smile and again felt guilty that she was not more attached to this woman. But if anybody wanted to adopt her she'd like it to be the Reids – but no, not the Reids - then Peter would become her brother which would ruin everything.

I must be in love with him, she thought.

"There is no need to mention to anybody about my offer to adopt you," Miss Langley said. "The nuns might be a little upset that I didn't ask them first, and we don't want to upset those good Sisters."

"I won't say anything," Elizabeth said.

One time when she was visiting Miss Langley, she saw a cigar case on the bureau. She picked it up and turned it over, seeing the initials M.H. inscribed on the silver bottom. Another time, she entered Miss Langley's room to look for a comb, as she had forgotten hers. The wardrobe door was hanging open and she saw what looked like a man's dressing gown hanging there. Surely a man was not staying overnight in the apartment! She must be mistaken.

"Oh, you see the dressing gown," Miss Langley was behind her and startled her a little. "Men's dressing gowns are much warmer than those for ladies so I bought myself a heavy flannel and ran one up to a pattern. Ladies' gowns are so light and summery, I do so find them inadequate in winter."

"Oh, of course," said Eliza. "I wasn't thinking –"

"Of course you weren't! Now, I have a scheme for us today. Let us go and find some new linens for your room. You must prefer living here to the convent, where the sheets are coarse and patched. You sleep better here, I'll warrant. And you need a new gown. The nuns never give you anything new."

Eliza knew that the nuns could not afford it, but it was true that she liked a new gown every so often. And she had grown to like her room in the apartment, it was comfortable and colourful unlike the very simple convent rooms and the bed was soft.

CHAPTER THIRTY-FIVE

S ister Anne came back for a visit. She was welcomed with open arms by everybody.

"Where is Elizabeth?" she asked, looking about. She was quite surprised to learn that Eliza was spending more and more time with Miss Langley. Of late, that lady could not go anywhere without her.

"I know I'm the suspicious type," she admitted. "But where does she get her money from?"

"She told me that she has inherited money," Mother Maria said. "And is living off the interest."

"Is Eliza very disappointed that she cannot enter the Order?"

"No, by the grace of God, she does not seem unhappy. Perhaps she knows deep down in her heart she is not meant for this life."

"Miss Langley takes her out and about with her. She has many friends. It would not surprise me if she were to fall in love. I would be very happy for her, if so," said Mother Maria.

Sister Clare sighed silently. She had hoped...but Miss Langley had introduced her to a life that was above that of a poor constable. Poor Peter would have to get over his broken heart!

CHAPTER THIRTY-SIX

It was March 1st 1888, and Miss Langley gave her 'niece' a pearl necklace and a new hat for her twenty-first birthday. Elizabeth thanked her very sincerely, though she was not even sure that March 1st was her birthday, not since Margaret had told her that Ethel had most likely been a charlatan. Eliza had never told Miss Langley her true opinion of her Blackpool friend. She thought that Miss Langley had been trying to do something nice for her and felt guilty that she had wasted money on nothing that day. The Sisters still celebrated her birthday on September 30th so she was in the amusing situation of having two birthdays. She noticed that Miss Langley never contradicted the Sisters when they continued to celebrate her birthday on that date. Miss Langley did not wish them to know that a fortune-teller had told her otherwise.

She was twenty-one years old today! The hat was very fetching and she drew admiring glances when she was out.

Miss Langley had been very quiet and almost reflective of late. Elizabeth felt that she had something on her mind.

"Will you come to London with me?" she asked abruptly later in the day.

"London!"

"Yes, for now you should be out in society, and we will meet many more people than we do here. I have friends and cousins in London. I would love them to meet you. They know all about you, you know. I've been telling them about you for years."

Again Eliza felt that odd dislike of Miss Langley that she had tried so many times to conquer. But she smiled and said:

"I must ask Mother Maria, and if she says yes, then I will."

"You're twenty-one years old now. You do not have to ask Mother Maria. She has given you into my custody this long time, and regards me as your guardian-in-fact. So I want to look after you."

"That's very kind of you, Aunt Laura. I'm quite overcome."

She had been calling her Aunt Laura for a few years now at Miss Langley's request. It felt awkward.

Miss Langley was both very nervous and excited at her years of work coming to an end. It had been a great situation, if tiresome at times. But two thousand pounds awaited her at the other end of the Lime Street to Euston railway line. She could retire comfortably on that if she invested it wisely. Freedom at last from educating the children of the rich! She would be genteel again.

CHAPTER THIRTY-SEVEN

Miss Langley did not care to visit Reids, there was nobody in the police inspector's house worth her notice. Eliza always visited on her own and as she never confided the secrets of her heart to her, Miss Langley was completely ignorant of the strong attachment between Elizabeth and Peter Reid. Had she known, it would have thrown her into a frenzy. If Elizabeth married, the money would be out of the grasp of the Mercers and they would cast her aside without the money she had been expecting. But she was quite happy to be rid of Elizabeth sometimes because she wanted to be with her friends, and she gave her a great deal of freedom.

As a young detective constable Peter did not have much time off. He still lived at home and the young sweethearts always met there or at Margaret's home.

This Sunday afternoon, they met at Margaret's and they felt like a long walk, so they went outside the city toward the picturesque village of Hale. It was a golden October day; the sun was shining and the air was mild and fresh.

"I'm going to London soon," Eliza said.

"London! Why?"

"Miss Langley is going and wishes me to go with her."

"Miss Langley! Elizabeth, you know how I feel about that woman. She's not an honest person. She gets my policeman's nose twitching, if you want the truth."

"I know, but she's fond of me and has given me a lot of nice things, and takes me out, and I feel I should repay her. And - I can't live at the convent anymore, they've done enough for me, and Miss Langley is the only - the only person I have."

"But when will you be back?"

"As soon as I can, Peter. I'm a Scouser, and I'll find as much fault with London as I can!"

"Before you go - I must speak - you know how I feel about you, Eliza."

"And you know how I feel about you, Peter."

They stopped walking and he took her hands in his.

"Now that you're all grown up, I can say this. I haven't said anything before because I haven't been in a position to offer you anything. But you're going away and I want you to know that I love you." She looked up at him with shining eyes, and he bent close to kiss her.

He had kissed her before but this time was different. She felt as if she were in danger of being carried off. The world around her fell away. She had never experienced feelings like these before. He prudently withdrew, smiling a little, and pressed her to his heart.

"Let's keep walking," he said, tucking her hand under his arm, his eyes alight with love. They walked on, close together and silent now, but no words were needed. The leaves whirled about them.

"So you're definitely not going to be a nun," he said.

"No. I accepted it and prayed and asked Jesus to show me the way - and it might have been a co-incidence, but just as I prayed, the doorbell rang, I answered and you were standing there. The sun was in my eyes and I could hardly see you for the light surrounding you! I knew then what He wanted!"

"You seemed a little dumbstruck at the time! So that was it?"

"Yes, and then I thought you'd never speak," she added with mischief.

"So – you're sure then?"

She nestled closer to him.

"I'm sure. Are you?"

"Yes, I am sure too. How will you like being married to a policeman, with odd hours and poor pay, except for reward money for solving crimes?"

"I hope I'd be a comfort to you, having your slippers warm by the fire when you come home and a hot bath. Oh! A home of my own, a real home!"

"It might be just two rooms to start off."

"I don't care...it will be a home and with the man I love."

"Shall we tell people we're engaged?"

"No, not yet. Wait until I get back from London, I'm sure I'll be gone only a few weeks."

"Don't stay any longer than that, my Eliza. If Miss Langley wants to stay longer, send me a message and I'll come and fetch you back! What part of London are you going to, anyway? It's a big place."

"She doesn't know yet, she said. But I'll write to you as soon as we're settled with her friends."

"That sounds vague." Peter frowned. "I must see you the evening before you go - may I?"

"Yes, I'm arranging the flowers in the church, so come there, will you?"

CHAPTER THIRTY-EIGHT

"As you're going to the church to arrange the flowers, dear, I wish you to do something for me," said Miss Langley. "I wish you to borrow Sister Clare's gold cross and chain, for I have a wish to look at it closely, I would like to have one made exactly like it, in London, so I wish to make notes or take a drawing."

"But you know Sister Clare is away. She's in Birmingham helping to set up the new Refuge. She won't be back before we go."

"You know her room well enough!"

"You want me to go and take it? Without asking her?"

"My dear I only want to borrow it. It sounds as if you don't trust me."

This made Eliza feel guilty so she went to the convent. Nobody minded her coming and going as she pleased, so she went in by the door in the church that led into the convent hallway, went upstairs and into Sister Clare's room. Nobody saw her.

She found the cross and chain and put it in her pocket, then wrote a note to Sister Clare explaining why she had taken it and telling her also that she had gone to London. She left, but shortly afterwards, the window of the room was opened by Sister Grace who wanted to air the room out. The breeze wafted Eliza's note from the bedside table and a series of other breezes caused it to end up behind the table and well out of sight.

Eliza went to the church to arrange the flowers. She was busy and happy, filled with a quiet joy that she knew came from doing God's will. The church door opened and Peter came in. He knelt, prayed a short prayer and she joined him. Hand in hand, they walked toward the altar and gazed upon the Tabernacle. They knelt, still hand in hand.

It was spontaneous, but there, they pledged themselves to each other before the Lord, with promises to love each other to the end of their lives, with His blessing upon them for all of their days. They walked down the aisle together, and said goodbye outside, and near the very steps where she had been found as a child, they kissed and parted, reluctantly.

My husband, she thought. *Not in law yet, but we have pledged ourselves before God's altar...*

CHAPTER THIRTY-NINE

"Here we are," said Miss Langley as they drew into Euston Station, the whistle announcing their approach. It was late at night. Everybody about them was getting up and gathering their bags, but she remained put.

"I hate to join the melee, everybody's in such a big hurry," Miss Langley said. She seemed fidgety as the train had approached their destination, and Eliza wondered if she were nervous about something. She said she'd been to London several times, so it couldn't be that. Elizabeth had been dreaming of Peter the entire journey to London, and Miss Langley had not even noticed that she was preoccupied and not at all excited about her first time in the most important city of the British Empire.

The train car was empty before they climbed down to an almost deserted platform. A man approached.

"Miss – er – Langley." He led the way down the dark platform, away from the direction that everybody else had taken. Eliza looked at Miss Langley with concern.

"Why are we going this way?" she asked, but she did not receive a reply.

They followed the platform until it was clear of buildings, and no more lights were used. It was very dark and deserted.

"This is very strange," whispered Eliza.

"It's all right," Miss Langley whispered back. "Just follow him." The man was joined by another man who appeared out of nowhere carrying a hurricane lamp. In the darkness, Elizabeth heard the neigh of a horse. They left the platform to a grassy area where a carriage awaited.

"Get in." Miss Langley said. Elizabeth obeyed.

"You've done well, Miss Shields," she heard the man's voice say. "Your duty is finished. My man will take you back up the platform and put you in a cab for your lodgings, where your final payment awaits you."

"Thank you," Elizabeth heard Miss Langley answer.

The man jumped into the carriage with her, and the door shut. He rapped on the ceiling and they lurched forward.

"Miss Langley! Miss Langley!" Eliza shouted her name with bewilderment and fright. But Miss Langley was left behind. What was happening? She tried the door handle to open it so she could jump out, but her wrist was caught by the stranger and he pushed her back on the seat.

"Miss Mercer," said he, "I am your Uncle, and you will do as I say."

"Miss Mercer? I'm not Miss Mercer! There's been a mistake!"

"That's your name. You're an heiress, Elizabeth Mary Mercer."

CHAPTER FORTY

She was in a large house, confined to a sort of cellar, downstairs in the servants' area, of whom, as far as she could tell, there were only two. But she had only been here for a day. The room had a bed, a table with a sewing machine on it, a chair and a chest of drawers with a jug and a basin. A door led to another room, but it was locked and bolted on the other side.

It was cold, even in summer.

My name is Mercer and I'm an heiress. The words played themselves over and over in her mind. *Mercer - heiress. Mercer - heiress.* It could not be true. And this man who said he was her uncle! Was he?

And why was Miss Langley, Miss Shields? Miss Langley had delivered her to these people; Miss

Langley was her enemy! Her cousin – the attorney who tried to set up the adoption – he was Shields!

Everything became a little clearer later when her uncle returned, this time with a woman who he introduced as her aunt. No first names were given.

"I believe you think you are from Scotland, and that your parents were poor crofters," said Aunt Mercer, seating herself on the one chair while her husband stood. Eliza was seated on the narrow bed. "It is not so," she continued.

"I knew that," said Eliza. "I knew that what the fortune teller told me was false."

"How did you know?"

"Because they are charlatans."

"You are a clever girl."

"Who is the woman I know as Miss Langley?"

The couple looked at each other.

"She was in our employ to form your character as you grew up. We sent her to visit you every day at the convent and then to take you to live with her."

She felt more angry than afraid. Having Peter by her side for life gave her courage and strength. How angry he would be when he found out all this! She'd borrow his anger for now.

"Did you abandon me near the convent when I was three years old, in the freezing cold?"

"Yes, but we knew you were in no danger. We were sorry, but you were much better off with the nuns than with us."

"We are cold people." said Uncle Mercer in a matter-of-fact way. "We are not nice people."

"Stop it, Anthony."

"You abandoned me cruelly! Was it you, both? Did you take me there to the convent, in thin rags and barefoot, so that I could have died of the cold? You didn't even cover me with a blanket!"

They had no response for her.

"Where are my parents?"

"They died in a boating accident some months before that. We are your legal guardians."

She mulled this fact for a moment. So her mother and father were dead. In spite of all the lies told to her about her origins, she believed this could be – was most probably true. Her parents were dead.

With the sad knowledge surged a more joyful thought - *they did not forsake her!*

"So they did not abandon me, as I thought," she said.

"You've had a happy life with the nuns, haven't you?" said her aunt brightly. "Miss Shields kept us up to date on your progress. And we met you once, you know, and were very pleased indeed at the modest, polite girl you were growing into. We were quite reassured as to your welfare."

Eliza thought of the loneliness of the years, the feeling of being abandoned and unloved by her own family. What was this wicked couple up to now?

"I'm not your prisoner, you have no right to keep me here, and I demand to leave now." Eliza said, jumping up. "You must put me on the next train to Liverpool."

"Impossible, until a certain meeting takes place next week," her uncle said. "You have to sign some papers, then you're free to go and do as you wish."

"Sign papers?"

"You have money since the day you turned twenty-one years old. We're your next-of-kin, and we'll manage it for you."

"On what day was it that I turned twenty-one years old?"

"March 1st, last."

How had the fortune-teller known that was her birthday? Because Miss Langley had told her. Miss Langley! She had told the fortune-teller what to say! What a thoroughly horrible woman she was! Mother Maria, how fooled you were! Sister Clare too! All of them, except Sister Anne, who did not like Miss Langley! And dear Peter! None of the Reids liked Miss Langley!

She asked a few more questions, such as her parents' names and ages, and asked to see a photograph, but was disappointed that there was none.

"We will leave you to think about it," said Uncle Mercer.

"And I heard that the nuns taught you how to sew. I will have some materials delivered. We've just moved to this house, and there are curtains to be sewn, and cushion covers and the like. I expect you'll like to be occupied."

"Who was Bridie?" she asked them before they left. "I remembered Bridie."

"She was your nursemaid."

Eliza remembered something else.

"You wanted the nuns to think I was a child from the rookeries," she said, unable to contain a little smirk. "They never did, for all the rags you put on me. Thanks to Bridie, I was clean and nourished and the soles of my feet were soft."

Mrs. Mercer looked aggravated, before she returned the smirk.

"It doesn't matter."

"Oh, but it does. When they hear about this, they'll go to the police. It's one thing for a desperately poor family to leave a child on their steps, but for someone rich to do it, putting my life at risk rather than trying to save it, as a poor family would intend – it might be a crime! Sister Clare comes from a family of Inspectors and Constables. Oh and another thing - Miss Langley never visited me every day - twice a month, if that."

"That's enough!" said Mrs. Mercer with anger, banging the door after her.

CHAPTER FORTY-ONE

"There's too much of Frank in her," said Mr. Mercer. "He was a spirited boy. We told Shields to knock the spirit out of her. But it seems she's prepared to put up a fight."

"That's very hazardous for us," said Mrs. Mercer. "One would wonder if it would just be better to – to –"

"To what?" Mr. Mercer frowned.

"We are her next-of-kin and legal guardians, it would come to us anyway," she said. "If anything happened to her."

"But it's complicated, Lydia. If she dies, it has to be publicly known in order for us to inherit; we have to identify her as Frank's daughter. Questions may be asked and these police constables may be low-class people but they are cunning as foxes. They smell crime."

"I thought you had more courage than that, Anthony."

"I'm not going to do it this time. Next thing, they'll start asking questions about the accident."

Mrs. Mercer was silent for a little while before she spoke again.

"We don't want that. And I agree with you about the police. There was a nosey Inspector at the time, I remember. If that boat were found, would they be able to tell that there was a little gash in one of the floorboards?"

"Hush!" Mr. Mercer looked as if he were about to jump out of his skin. "But we only speak like this because she has demonstrated obstinacy. It should have gone very smoothly for us. We have waited for so long for this day! Miss Shields failed in forming her character."

"I'm very angry with Shields. She was supposed to visit daily, and instead she spent our money doing exactly what she wanted! Have we settled with her in full, Anthony?"

"I'm afraid so."

"We will get it back."

CHAPTER FORTY-TWO

Eliza was in a morose, pessimistic mood. The servants - an old man and an old woman - were kind but hardly spoke to her. She was unable to leave the cellar, let alone the house. It was a week now.

She was desperate to write to Peter, but had not even a pencil. She was truly a prisoner –

worse, because prisoners had the right to communicate with their loved ones. Her head could not contain all of her thoughts – all she wanted to tell him!

She understood it all now. The first few days she thought she would go and sign whatever they wanted, just to get out and get back to Liverpool and to Peter. She did not care about the money. She had never had money in her life and did not have a desire for it. But after a few days, she saw the evils of doing as they wanted.

She did not want them to reap the harvest of their wicked ways. And she had surges of affection for her dead parents, who had provided for her in such a way that she would have money setting out in life. She wanted to honour them. It had been their will for her. Had they known how avaricious her legal guardians would be in the event of their deaths? It was very possible.

She decided to resist. She had nothing else to do but sew, and she did that with rebellion toward her Mercer relatives in her heart. She sewed cushion covers all the way around, and crooked seams on the drapes. She made a gown for herself out of a material meant for curtains – a nice floral design - why should she not? They had not provided her with any garments, and her luggage had disappeared! It was a little cold, so a length of thick blue velvet cloth was made into a voluminous shawl.

She thought of Peter all the time, thought of their beautiful kiss, and longed with all her heart to see him again and to feel his arms wrap around her. He would wonder by now why she had not written!

At last the door opened to admit her uncle and aunt.

"What have you been doing?" her aunt asked sharply, looking around. The gown was draped over the chair and the velvet shawl covered her bed.

"I have been occupying myself, as you see."

Her aunt took up a cushion cover and turned it several times. "Where is the opening? You have no opening!"

"Oh dear! I must have gotten carried away!"

The couple were very angry - and nervous, she thought. She was very nervous also but tried to hide it. She wondered if her ploy would work.

"Have you decided to sign?" her uncle demanded.

"Oh, yes."

"Yes?" she could feel their relief spread from them. They exhaled.

"It is a pretty gown," said her aunt, taking up the material. "You have talent, my girl."

"But there may be a problem," she went on, her heart beating so fast she could almost hear it.

"What is it?"

"I'm married."

She would have enjoyed the silence that ensued, if it were not a sin to tell a lie.

"You are lying," said her aunt.

"I'm not lying," (*God forgive me! But am I not as good as married? Before your altar, did Peter and I not pledge ourselves to each other?*)

"What is his name? Why does Miss Shields not know of this?" asked Aunt Mercer.

"He is Detective Constable Peter Reid." (Did Mr. Mercer start, and grow pale?) "Miss Shields does not know because I did not tell her and she dislikes the Reid family who she has always considered beneath her. I never told her I loved Peter and he loved me. We married the evening before I left for London. It was a secret, so I do not wear a ring."

Mr. Mercer appeared to be shaking with fear, or was it anger? He went to the small window from where there was nothing to be seen but the grassy slope upwards, and drew his hands through his hair. He shifted from foot to foot. Then a sound came from him like that of an enraged bull.

Mrs. Mercer was pale with rage.

"Where did you marry?"

"Liverpool, at the convent, privately."

"I don't believe you."

She shrugged her shoulders.

"I am Mrs. Reid, and Peter is my next-of-kin."

Mrs. Mercer rose.

"These matters can be checked. I will send to Liverpool immediately."

Mr. Mercer turned his head around. His brow was moist and he was breathing hard. They swept out.

A little while later, her carpet-bag was thrown into her room. She took it as a good sign.

CHAPTER FORTY-THREE

"We have to leave it now, Lydia, cut our losses and get out. We'll go abroad."

"No, she's lying! We'll send a man to Liverpool to check the marriage registers!"

"Leave it, Lydia! Did you not hear her say the name *Reid*? Inspector Reid? He was the policeman who wanted the boat raised, and I had to pay a city official to get the matter dropped! She married *Reid's son, or nephew*! I'm as good as hanged!"

"Don't be cowardly! We will not leave it! She's lying! I haven't worked so hard, for so long, laying out thousands of pounds to Shields, only to walk away now! I'm going to see her this very day to get that money back."

"It's all right for you," Anthony said bitterly. "They'll hardly think you were the one who took a hatchet to the boat. *No, that's the man, the brother. We'll hang him.* But if I go down, you're coming down with me. I'll make sure of it!"

"I'll deny everything!"

"You left the child on the convent steps!"

"That's not murder! That's - I don't know. I'll say you forced me."

"I will kill you first! If I hang for two murders why not three?"

Mrs. Mercer took a cab to Miss Shields's lodgings and was surprised to find that she was not alone - a man was there who was introduced to her as Mr. Heppleworth, and he appeared to be quite at home, seated casually on a sofa in a smoking jacket. However, when he realised that Mrs. Mercer wished for a private conversation with Miss Shields, he removed himself to another room.

Stinging over her vicious quarrel with her husband, Mrs. Mercer was boiling with fury.

"I have a number of grievances, Miss Shields. Firstly, that Miss Mercer is as obstinate as a mule and impertinent and angry. She's not at all the malleable creature you led me to believe you had fashioned. She's like a caged lion. She has told us some very interesting things, including the fact that far from you visiting her every day at the convent, it was more like once or twice a month! I paid you to go every day to see to her character! No wonder you failed!"

"So what of it? Have you any idea what convents are like? Quiet, boring, holy places. She was a meek mousey girl who loved animals. I couldn't stand her! How I wanted to beat her instead of pretending to be her friend! As for you accusing me of not molding her, I will prove that she does everything I say. The day before we left for London, I prevailed upon her to steal a valuable item from Sister Clare's room. A cross and chain. Easy!"

"But that's not all! Have you ever heard of a Detective Constable Peter Reid?"

"Well, yes, he's Sister Clare's nephew."

"WHY were you not aware of a growing attachment between Elizabeth and Mr. Reid?"

"An attachment? That's ridiculous. It could not be!"

"Yes, there is an attachment! More than an attachment! She claims to be married to him!"

"No, that cannot be true. She is not married, I assure you."

"She says they were married in the convent chapel the night before she left for London."

"Not true. She's telling lies."

"How do you know? Were you with her all the time?"

"No, she did go to the convent, as I said, to steal the cross and chain."

"It appears that as well as stealing the cross and chain, she found the time to run into the chapel and get married. If this turns out to be true, I will ruin you! You will not have a penny to bless yourself with! You'll have to go down to Whitechapel and sell yourself to that Ripper, or whatever they call him! And I hope you will be his next victim! And – I want our money back, give it to me now."

"I can't. It's in the bank."

"I will come here tomorrow and you had better have it! Good day to you!"

She left. Mr. Heppleworth emerged from the other room. Miss Shields was pale. She sat down abruptly on the sofa.

"What was that, Maggie? I never heard such an angry woman in my life!"

"It's a big misunderstanding, Michael. Nothing to concern ourselves with. Pour me a gin, would you? I'm in need of one. Whitechapel indeed!"

"You never did tell me why you called yourself Miss Langley in Liverpool. Sometimes I think you're a dark horse, Maggie. Who was that woman? Was she talking about Elizabeth?"

"Gin, Michael! Please! Gin!"

CHAPTER FORTY-FOUR

No post today either. It was extremely peculiar. He did not doubt Eliza's love for him, but why was there no letter?

Miss Langley. Of course - she who exerted so much influence over Elizabeth. She had something to do with it.

He went to the convent after work. His aunt Clare was back, and she was puzzled.

"She's gone to London?" she said. "I thought she would have left me a note!"

"She was here the evening before she left, arranging the flowers in the church," he replied, the memory fresh and pleasing.

"Something else is odd. My cross and chain is gone. Gone from my top drawer where I always keep it. It must have been stolen."

The policeman in her nephew was alert.

"Do you want to make a report, Aunt?"

"No."

"Why not? Because one of the girls here might have taken it?"

"Because – the only person who knew where it was, was Elizabeth."

"Oh, Aunt Clare. No, she couldn't have taken it."

"I don't think so either. And if she had, she'd have left me a note. Did you know she was going to London, Peter?"

"Yes, I saw her the evening before." He smiled at the memory, but said no more.

"I suppose we shall hear from her soon. She'll write to me, and I will let you know when I hear."

"Thank you, Aunt." But Peter privately thought that he should hear long before Aunt Clare! He and Eliza were married in their hearts if not officially!

"I know we do not read the newspapers in here, but we have heard rumours of an insane killer on the loose in London," Sister Clare said. "Such a wicked world!"

Peter had a calm and reasoned personality; he knew that it was highly unlikely that Miss Langley and Eliza were even near Whitechapel. He reassured his aunt of that fact and then left.

Though he ruled 'Jack the Ripper' out from having anything to do with Eliza's silence, he became seriously concerned, and one person in all of her affairs never left his mind - Miss Langley. She was the scowling woman angry to be discovered taking Eliza to a fortune-teller, the cold woman who always ignored him, as if he were not worth her notice or perhaps she feared him – the woman who was a major influence over Eliza's mind and heart. Mother Maria was taken in by her and encouraged the association, and Eliza herself felt guilty because she did not like Miss Langley as Miss Langley liked her. But Peter knew that Miss Langley was not fond of Eliza. It was a massive pretense. Why?

Why indeed? Did it have something to do with her past? As he wrote up a report that evening on a burglary, one resolve surged above all others in his mind – he was going to find out who Miss Elizabeth Snowe was, once and for all.

There was no time to be lost, so he could not wait for his days off. He wrote for the information right away using police stationery.

A few days later, more alarmed than ever at the continued silence from London, he was rewarded with a reply to his enquiry.

Dear Constable, with reference to your letter inst, we have located the birth record of an infant female to Mr. Francis Mercer and his wife Barbara, on March 1st 1867, at their address in 40 Glenwilliam Street, Knotty Ash, Liverpool. The child was named Elizabeth Mary.

She was a Liverpudlian, and Knotty Ash was a posh area.

Now to find the Mercers!

He would go there in person, of course, and set out there that very day after work.

A wealthy area, so was Elizabeth of the servant or upper class? It could be either, the fact that she was clean and vermin-free did not mean that her parents were wealthy, it only meant that they were clean, careful people, not living in the slum or unable to care for their child. Ah! Number 40! A fine modern house, red-brick with gabled windows in front, with trees in the garden.

The present occupants had only been there two years, and were very apologetic that they had no knowledge about the Mercers, but he could enquire of the servants. One handyman, Richard, had worked in the house for a long time.

Richard was a man about sixty, and remembered the Mercers well.

They're the people who drowned in the boating accident, very tragic. Lovely people! They had a little girl. She was supposed to go with them that day, you know? But she had a cold. After their deaths, she went to her uncle and aunt, yes, Mr. Mercer's older brother - much older, stepbrother. Yes, I knew where they lived then, but they moved from there, and bought an estate called Southall - no, not that, it was Sour - no, not that either, what was it - dang the memory! With age, it happens - Sackhall. Yes, Sackhall. They came into a lot of money. Other servants here at the time? There was Julia O'Hara and Bridie Ryan, she was nursemaid to the girl. Yes, Bridie. She married a butler named Forster, they're in service in Yew Tree. Did I tell you the Mercers came into a lot of money?

Forster in Yew Tree. When he returned home that evening, it was about eleven o'clock, and his father and mother were still up. His father was Detective Chief Inspector and when Peter told his story and came to the boating accident, he banged his fist on the table, shaking the cups.

"I went to the scene to investigate! A boat hand reported to me that he had seen a chap coming out of the boathouse that morning, when he had no business to be there. He carried something under his coat, and looked about him before he took off on foot. The boat hand also found a pan belonging to *The Eliza*. That's the pan to bail out the boat. It had been removed. I made my report and intended to go out and get the boat up, but an order came from above that I was to drop all further enquiries. It seemed to me to be a bit odd that an experienced yachtsman went out in a boat that sank like a stone twenty minutes later, and no squall, not a breath of wind, and nothing to bail out a leak on board. An investigation was warranted. And then there was all that money his brother got. I was very angry, I can tell you!"

"I remember that too!" cried Mrs. Reid. "But where is poor Eliza now, Peter? We hear such terrible things about London nowadays, no woman is safe there! I think you'll have to go to London to find her! "

"As for the Mercers," continued his father, 'I'll go to the Superintendent first thing in the morning and if he doesn't hear me, I'll go higher still. They're going to re-open that case! And I have friends in the Yard, Peter, I'll write a few letters tonight for you to take in the morning."

CHAPTER FORTY-FIVE

Peter set himself up in lodgings near Scotland Yard, and introduced himself to the detectives there.

"Your fame comes ahead of you," a desk sergeant said as he handed him a telegraph.

MERCERS MOVED-STOP-BOUGHT LONDON HOUSE-STOP-STAND BY FOR ADDRESS.STOP.

Peter outlined the entire story to Chief Detective Parsons. He mentioned the woman Miss Langley, and how she had brought Miss Mercer to London. He was convinced that this was a case of kidnap.

"'Ang on a sec, mate" a young detective interrupted, coming over. "We know something about the names Langley and Mercer. A report was filed by the lover of a Miss Shields, who also goes by Langley, saying she robbed him and made away with all he 'ad. A strange story – the plaintiff reported that this Miss Shields or Langley was governess to a Miss Snowe, Elizabeth Snowe, and one day, he was in her lodgings - and a very angry woman called Mrs. Mercer visited and berated Miss Shields for not bringing Miss Snowe up the way she wanted her brought up. She was not at all the creature she was supposed to be, and she said she was married to boot, and Miss Shields did not know anything about that."

Peter sat up straight, several sensations fighting to make themselves known in his mind and heart.

"Married!" he exclaimed, not knowing what to think at first.

"Married the night before she left Liverpool."

Peter smiled broadly, his heart soaring.

"A clever girl," he said, full of secret glee.

"So Mrs. Mercer threatened to ruin Miss Shields, and so she took fright, and one mornin' when the plaintiff woke up, she'd gone, cleanin' him out, left 'im with nothing."

"Good grief!"

"We found 'er at the ferryport, making away for France."

"You mean - you have her? In custody?"

"Oh yeah, of course we do. We're good, mate. Telegraph to all the Ports, she was nabbed."

"Miss Snowe and Miss Mercer are the same lady. But does Shields know where she is?"

"We asked her about that, wantin' to question her as well, and she said no, she says that at Euston late at night, they were attacked, and Miss Shields was knocked to the ground, and Miss Snowe - Mercer you say - was not there when she came to."

"I'd like to interview Miss Shields," Peter said. "And I need to know the address of this house that the Mercer couple bought the moment it comes in. I think Elizabeth - Miss Mercer - may be in grave danger."

Peter was young, but he impressed the Scotland Yard detectives with his penetrative mind, his clarity, quickness and his eagerness to get the case solved. He saw nothing but this case, and was not interested in anything London had to offer by way of amusement, at least not until he found the missing

Miss Mercer. He already spoke with authority. They liked this bright Limey. Perhaps they could recruit him, but for now, they'd help him as much as they could.

CHAPTER FORTY-SIX

"Miss Shields." Peter was shown into her cell in the Bridewell.

"It's Peter Reid." She swivelled her eyes in contempt.

"Detective Reid, if you please. I am here on police business."

"You're not wearing your uniform."

"I have some questions for you, Miss Shields." He tapped his pencil on his notebook.

"And I for you. Are you married to Miss Snowe?"

"I'm asking the questions. Where's Elizabeth?"

Miss Shields said that she did not know, and after some minutes more Peter was inclined to believe her. She tried to tell him the cock-and-bull story of being attacked at Euston, but under closer scrutiny admitted that she had delivered Miss Snowe - Mercer - to her uncle there. After that, she never saw Elizabeth again.

"My life was threatened by the Mercers. You have to protect me. I'm quite frightened of them. I think they killed his brother for the money."

"That's a Liverpool matter. I'm here to find Miss Mercer."

"You've never liked me, Peter Reid. That day you saw me in Blackpool, I didn't like the look you gave me."

"Nor I the look you gave me. Despicable to take a nine-year-old to a fortune-teller, just to give yourself more power over her. I was only a boy but I knew what you were doing. Babs and Bridie being the same name and all that."

"What?"

"I was around the back, my head inside the tent."

He heard his name called from the guard on duty. Perhaps the address had come!

"But are you married to Elizabeth?" she called after him as he left, banging the cell door in frustration.

He made no reply.

"The wonder of the telegraph," said the old desk sergeant, as he handed him the slip of paper.

"That's nothing," said another, young constable, unconsciously grooming the edge of his heavily-waxed moustache. "Soon we'll have Bell Telephones. We'll be able to talk to each other, you in the Yard, me at a police station twenty miles away."

"I hope I'm gone afore then," said the sergeant. "That ain't natural, no, it ain't. Like the whistles we have to use now. Anybody can have a whistle, but the policeman's rattle, everybody knew that."

Peter had heard none of the exchange. He had the address of the house that the Mercers had bought.

CHAPTER FORTY-SEVEN

In Liverpool, the house and estate at Sackhall was shut up. Only a caretaker was there, and he did not look in the least surprised to see the police at the door.

"Have you come on behalf of the bank?" he asked.

Chief Inspector Reid drew his own conclusions from the comment. He asked to take a look around the rooms shrouded in dust-covers and sheets. He and his team of two constables opened drawers and cupboards and wardrobes, but the couple had truly gone, packed up everything and left for their new home. They had not left a scrap of paper or a photograph behind. There was nothing to be found here, no incriminating evidence at all.

Mrs. Bridie Forster, nee Ryan, was now in service with her husband to the Greenlea family in Yew Tree. The Chief put them at ease and they sat in the servant's hall. As his mission became known, and Elizabeth's story, Bridie's eyes misted over until she was weeping into the corner of her apron.

"Is that what she did? And I thought she was going to be kind to her, I did. She got rid of her the minute I was gone out the door. The poor little child!"

Bridie could not tell him anything of great worth to the reopened case. She was very upset indeed.

"I have a photo of her with her Mama and Papa," she said, getting up and leaving them. He heard her steps on the back stairs, and within a few minutes she was back again, with a card wrapped up in an old yellowed handkerchief and tied with blue ribbon.

"When you find her, I want her to 'ave this, please" she said, pressing it into his hands.

"I'll send it to my son forthwith," he promised. "And we're doing everything we can to find her."

"So she might 'ave been that little girl at the fortune-teller." Bridie said to her husband later.

CHAPTER FORTY-EIGHT

Barkelly House was a mansion on its own extensive grounds on the far side of Chelsea. It was several miles from the railway station and in a very quiet road with few neighbours. Peter walked around the perimeter wall of old stone, its crevices sprouting leaves and weeds, looking for a back way in. He was in plain clothes, dressed as a labourer.

His father wrote that the Sackhall Estate was in hock up to its chimneys, and Peter considered that the Mercers must have got a loan for this place on the strength of the eighty thousand pounds they expected to get soon.

Around the back, he found a large iron gate. It led down a wide lane past several sheds, a large greenhouse filled with nursery pots of fir trees, drooping for want of water. A Christmas tree farm! Planted in the open were the bigger trees, some half-grown, others up to ten feet high, and he wondered, with Christmas around the corner, why nobody was there to chop them down to take to the markets. He had learned that the previous owner of the house had died suddenly, leaving no children, and the heir lived in Sheffield. He had put the house immediately up for sale.

Peter wondered how much interest the new owners had in their Christmas tree farm. Probably none. The attraction of this secluded house was that the owner wanted a quick sale so they got it at a bargain price.

The residence was not far away and the trees almost backed up to it, so taking a route among them he neared the back of the old house of grey stone.

"What do you want?" He spun about to see a bullish man of middle age seated upon a horse, scowling at him. By his dress, he was either the steward or Mercer himself.

"Oh, sorry guv'nor," he hid his Scouse accent and had gleaned enough of the south of England accent to pass as a local man. He whipped off his cap. "I was passin' by the gate out there and knew there was a Christmas tree farm, and I'm idle at the moment, and I was in hopes of gettin' a job, if you need somebody to cut 'em down? I came in in 'opes of seein' the 'Ead Gardener."

The man scrutinised him.

"We do not have a gardener, head or otherwise. We just moved in. We haven't got round to engaging all of our staff."

"Well, guv'nor, whenever you do, I'd be grateful for your consideration. My name is Thomas Black, everybody round 'ere knows me as Tom B."

"I do not think we need anybody until spring, perhaps."

"That's a pity, guv'nor, for if you don't mind my sayin' so, these trees here are ready to be cut down for the Christmas market. They won't be arf as good next year. They'll be too 'igh for the average house. And those ones in the green'ouse - I couldn't 'elp seein', they won't be fit to be planted out come spring if they aren't watered regular throughout the winter, and they are – or were – 'ealthy young saplings. They're arf-dead. Some pot-bound too. Those plants are worth a lot of money, I'd say."

"Are they? How much?"

"Several 'undred pounds by my reckonin'. A pity to lose 'em, for the sake of a bit of waterin' every now and then."

The man appeared to consider this. Peter wondered if he should encourage him more, but he did not wish to appear too keen. He made one step backwards.

"Don't go," said Mr. Mercer. "When can you start?"

"Today, if you like, guv'nor. I'll begin by savin' those plants in the green'ouse, and tommerer I can chop the mature ones. I know a chap with a market in Covent Garden, he'd buy 'em from you at a good price."

"Very well, Tom B. You may contact your friend and we shall agree a price. As to your conditions of employment, you will not be a part of the household, but rather come on a day to day basis, until we see how you get on. I'll pay you by the day, because if it rains, I daresay you won't come at all. Sixpence a day and I expect ten hours. Bring your lunch, and don't go into the house. You can get water from the pump in the yard."

"That will be – *very good*, sir." Tom pretended to look disappointed and unwilling to accept the paltry sum too readily. It was an insult to offer one's labour for that with no dinner or accommodation. What a penny-pincher this man was! "To whom do I 'ave the honor of speaking, sir, if I might ask?"

"Mr. Mercer, Mr. Anthony Mercer. I am the owner."

"I'm very pleased to meet you, sir, and grateful for the employment, just afore Christmas too, we'll 'ave a good Christmas after all, the wife will be that 'appy when I tells 'er, she will."

With that, they parted, Mr. Mercer with a stiff, unsmiling nod, and Peter with a subservient bow before he planted his cap back on his head.

CHAPTER FORTY-NINE

By now, Eliza had almost given up hope of being found. She awoke every morning to the same scene, the dull, and now very cold room. Water was brought to her and then her breakfast was handed in – a plate of thinly buttered bread and a cup of weak tea. The woman who brought it looked at her with a mixture of pity and alarm. When she had asked her desperately one morning if she would give her a pen and paper she shook her head with vehemence and threw her eyes to the ceiling, as if in reference to Upstairs.

After dressing, Eliza got down to work. She sewed and sewed and sewed. Her initial bravado in sabotaging her tasks and confiscating materials for her own use ebbed soon after as the reality of her situation gradually sank in. Now she knew that sewing was saving her life, or at least her sanity. Curtains and drapes and table linens and gowns.

Dinner was a thin soup with a few pieces of potato and carrots or cabbage floating in it. She was given a slice of bread after it and a cup of tea. The afternoon was spent with more sewing. Her supper was gruel and dry bread and tea.

She was hungry. And she would become even more so, because Mrs. Mercer had told her that she would starve if she did not sign her fortune over to them. But Elizabeth was resolute on that point. Her parents would not want her to give in. She was sure of it, as sure as if they were in the room advising her.

She thought of Peter all the time. Where was he? Would he think that she jilted him because she did not write? Would he think she met another man in London? Would he think she regretted her pledge made in front of the altar the evening before she left Liverpool? She longed for him. She sent her guardian angel with messages for him but she did not know if that worked or not. Did she even have a guardian angel? She doubted everything now.

What of Sister Clare? Where was that gold cross and chain now? She had promised to bring it back and she had not returned it.

She was sure she was a grave disappointment to everybody who had been good to her. As far as they were concerned, she'd absconded with Miss Langley and was being danced off her feet at Christmas parties and balls.

As the weather became colder the tips of her fingers became numb and clumsy when trying to thread the needle and do other tasks that needed precise movements. But this room did not have a fireplace. It was evidently part of another room that had been partitioned. She wrapped herself in her blankets even during the day.

CHAPTER FIFTY

M r. and Mrs. Mercer were hardly on speaking terms. They disagreed as to how they should proceed. There was no marriage between Reid and Elizabeth and they, the Mercers, were indeed her next-of kin.

Mrs. Mercer wanted her introduced to a few friends as their niece, and then get rid of her – a tragic accident, a period of mourning, then they could go abroad – for good. Mr. Mercer was adamantly against the scheme. To inherit a fortune once by accident was enough, but twice? Even their friends would raise eyebrows.

They were at an impasse. Mealtimes were angry times.

"What do you suggest? Do you have a better idea? Because I can't think of one. If only Miss Shields had not failed us so miserably!" Mrs. Mercer said with a biting air.

"Miss Shields did not fail us as much as you failed us. *You* failed us miserably. If you had kept her with us, instead of farming her out, the natural bond of affection between you both would have resulted in you being able to easily persuade her. We're strangers to her – that's the problem! She does not love or trust us!" He was shouting now.

"Don't put the blame on me! You are the relation, not me! I didn't see you object to our giving her away, did you?"

"I mentioned a school, did I not?"

Outside in the hallway, old Mr. Blaine took his hand from the doorknob and went downstairs again.

"Are they ready for dessert?" his wife asked.

"All the sugar in the world wouldn't sweeten those two."

"Oh don't tell me they're at it again."

"Hell for leather at it. Something very fishy going on. It's to do with the lass."

"Why are we not allowed to speak with her?"

"My hearing is not too good but they sent her out to be reared and whoever it was did a bad job."

"I think she is a very nice young woman; very well-mannered and tidy and says her prayers. I don't believe the story Her Ladyship gave us, of her havin' eloped and they got her back in time and put her in there for a while to make her forget her lover. And I don't feel right about our part in it."

"They're so rich and they hate each other," Mr. Blaine mused. "whereas you and I, Mrs. Blaine, we don't have much, but you're still the rosy-cheeked dimpled damsel I married forty years ago."

"Joshua Blaine, get away from me! Now is not the time for stealing kisses!" she swatted him playfully with a spoon. He laughed, and turned toward the window.

"Who is that fellow crossing the yard? Look!"

"He's the gardener. He's here to cut down Christmas trees and you and I are going to have to decorate one and put it in the Hall."

"We need the spirit of Christmas in this house," Mr. Blaine remarked.

The dining-room bell rang, and it seemed to have an angry sound.

"I suppose they are ready," he said with a sigh.

CHAPTER FIFTY-ONE

Sister Clare received the news from her brother that the Mercers were criminals and that Miss Langley had been in their employ. It fell to her to tell Mother Maria, who at first could not believe her, but then broke down and wept.

"I was so foolish! I was blind! Just because she could speak Italian and I was homesick to hear it! I should have listened to Anne! Oh, God forgive me! And now, where is poor Elizabeth?"

Sister Clare comforted her as best she could, saying that she, too had been deceived. Afterwards, she went to her room and sank down on the bed. She had a headache. As she turned her head on the pillow, she saw a piece of paper caught between the back of the bedside table and the wall. She reached out and took it.

Dear Sister Clare, Miss Langley sent me to fetch your gold cross and chain to her as she wishes to make a drawing of it to get one made for herself. I was very reluctant to take it without your permission, but she was so insistent that you would not mind, so I'm borrowing it. I will take great care of it, Love Eliza. PS I will write you from London.

Poor Eliza! The influence that woman had over you! Where are you now, my little motherless child?

She slipped to her knees and began to pray.

CHAPTER FIFTY-TWO

'Tom B' was not about to spend any more time in the greenhouse than he could help. The next morning he set off with a hatchet to chop trees. He had never chopped a tree in his life but that did not disturb him. His intention was to find the lay of the land for an operation, a rescue, if he discovered that Eliza was in this house. And she probably was.

A row of young evergreens bordered the house on the rear, and it was to these that he went, the hatchet in hand, as if ready to strike if Mr. Mercer should come along to see what he was doing. Perhaps he should chop a few to make it look as if he was working.

Chopping trees was much more difficult than he supposed! He was using muscles he did not even know he had in his back and his upper arms, and he was a fit young man, as policemen have to be, to pursue criminals, defend themselves when attacked, and restrain a strong man long enough to get handcuffs on. He exercised every morning with the other men.

Thankfully Mr. Mercer did not appear to see his clumsiness. At last, a tree crashed to the ground, and in the right direction, away from him.

He chopped a few more down and then thought he had enough done to show some labour so he walked about a little. He walked around the house towards the back until he came to the poultry yard, empty of fowl, the kitchen garden and the back door leading to the scullery and kitchen. He walked toward the stables and saw two young horses, one of which was Mr. Mercer's mount of the day before. The horses were strong and he supposed, fleet of foot. The coach house was nearby and a carriage waited there. Following a path from the coach house, he came to another large back gate. This led onto a laneway only a quarter of a mile from the main road away from town.

If anybody wanted to get away in a hurry, this is the road they would take. He walked back to the greenhouse, thinking. He had to bring this quickly to an end.

Back at Scotland Yard that evening, he opened a packet from his father. A letter, and a card wrapped carefully in a handkerchief tied with ribbon.

The letter was to tell him the developments in Liverpool with the urging to act quickly at his end. He opened the wrapped card and though he was a man with his feelings under control, he swallowed when he saw the portrait of the small family group, a young father and mother sitting on the rug in front of a Christmas tree, their little daughter between them. The mother was another Elizabeth, but he could see Eliza in her father too, the tilt of her nose was his. The child was looking shyly at the camera, an intimidating object perhaps – blissfully innocent of the cruel turn her life would take. The couple expected decades of Christmases' to come and go and most likely adding to their numbers in future photos. His heart sorrowed for all of them. After staring at it for some time, he wrapped it carefully again and put it in his inside pocket.

He took a pencil and a sheet of paper and from memory sketched the house and its surroundings. Then on a separate sheet, he formulated a plan.

CHAPTER FIFTY-THREE

What was that noise? Eliza stopped her sewing machine to listen. Somebody was working outside, she heard thuds and chops and rustlings. It was frustrating that all she could see from the window, beyond the bars, was a steep ditch. Nevertheless, she could try to get the person's attention - it was most likely a man working out there, but perhaps it was only the old man she had glimpsed every now and then with the old woman.

It was most likely him. She went back to her sewing, working the treadle with her feet.

Outside, Peter was chopping as many trees as he could, for Mr. Mercer had come along and snapped at him, saying he wasn't worth the money he was spending on him and had he contacted that fellow from Covent Garden? Peter was as humble and apologetic as he could be, saying that he'd written to him to tell him to come out and see Mr. Mercer as soon as ever he could, and that he'd work harder today, to have as many trees cut down for him as possible, fine trees they were.

Mr. Mercer rode away and Peter threw his axe away. In the quiet, he thought he heard an unusual noise. A whirr coming from one of the basement rooms. He walked closer in its direction.

In the kitchen, Blaine smirked to his wife, "That new fellow is no gardener."

"What? How do you know?" She picked up a basin of raw potatoes to take them to the table to peel.

"Yesterday, I watched him from an upstairs window, snoopin' around."

Mrs. Blaine's face lit up. She set the heavy basin on the table with a thud and took a potato up to peel it.

"That's her lover, then! He came to rescue her!" She said, paring more peel from the potato than she meant to.

"What an imagination women have! He's a horse stealer, I saw him around the stables."

Mrs. Blaine wasn't listening. "We should help him, Joshua. Go on out and tell him we know everything, and ask him in for a mince pie at eleven. I'm going in to take one in to Miss Mercer and tell her everything will be all right from now on. I can't bear to see her suffer any more."

"I pray you do no such thing. Our wages will be withheld if Madam Upstairs suspects we're being nice to her."

"Oh! All right."

Blaine shuffled outside in the direction of the gardener, and was not pleased to see him standing and staring at the very spot where the girl was being kept. Maybe Mrs. Blaine was right after all!

"What you doin' here, lad? An't you supposed to be cutting a Christmas tree? Why're you snooping around where you've got no business?"

CHAPTER FIFTY-FOUR

Peter was at first annoyed with himself for being caught. He looked keenly at the old man. This could blow it all up before he was ready to act.

He reached into his inner pocket and took out his police badge.

"Don't say ought. I'm Detective Constable Reid from Liverpool and I'm here on police business. I need help getting into this house."

Mr. Blaine was astonished.

"Why?" he asked, a little suspiciously.

"I will tell you, but first I want to ask you how long you know the Mercers."

"Only a short time. We came with the house, my wife and I."

Peter was glad to hear this. He did not have to deal with a loyal retainer, some of whom would prefer to be shot rather than see their family in trouble.

"The Mercers are wanted on suspicion of very serious crime, murder and kidnapping."

Blaine drew back in horror.

"You must help me before these people commit another murder," he added quickly.

"Of course, sir, I mean – Detective –"

"No, no, I'm Tom. Tom Black the gardener. The kidnap victim is in that room, is she not?" He pointed to the window below.

"Yes, and she's in a poor state. Is it true she eloped? That's what we were told."

"No, not true at all. They're after the money left to her by her parents."

"Ooooh, I see. I'm Joshua Blaine, er – Tom."

"Here's what we'll do, Blaine. We'll take one of those trees I cut into the house. I'll be Tom the gardener of course and speak like a Tom the gardener. You've got to direct me and speak to me sharp, understand? I promise you I shall not mind in the least if you shout and curse at me like I was the clumsiest oaf around. Don't give me away, that I will mind."

Blaine agreed, and they went to the cut trees and chose a large one for the house. Since it was going into the Hall, it made no sense to bring it in the back, so Blaine went to the kitchen to ask his wife to open the front door. He took his time and Peter began to wonder, until he reappeared.

"I told Mrs. Blaine as well," he said. "So she goes along with us. She reads Sherlock Holmes."

"Let's get on, then." Peter said, a trifle impatient.

Mrs. Mercer came downstairs as they were setting it up in the Hall.

"Oh, there it is. Isn't there any better one there?"

"This is the best one, Madam."

"I'm sure there are better, but this new man just doesn't want the bother of cutting it down. Anthony!"

Her husband came downstairs and she pointed to the tree.

"Tell him to go and cut down a better tree than that scraggly object!"

"My wife is correct. Tom B, take that thing away. Did your friend arrive yet?"

"He's to be 'ere very soon, sir."

"Very well. How many have you cut for him?"

"About two dozen or thereabouts, sir."

They carried the tree out and Blaine whispered when they were out of earshot, "When are you going to – er – act, er, Tom?"

"Patience yet. I have a better idea than the one I had – safer. I'm going to start something, and I want you to take me on. Lock me up in the boot room or somewhere, so that they will call the Police. I have several men at the station in Chelsea waiting for a signal to come out here. You and Mrs. Blaine secure me well. Manhandle me."

"If you say so, er – Tom!"

Out of sight of the house, Peter took his badge and placed it inside his vest. But he forgot the packet tied with the handkerchief.

CHAPTER FIFTY-FIVE

This tree was satisfactory, and they set it upright and set about decorating it.

"Why are you hanging about, Tom?" Mrs. Mercer said. "You go out and cut more trees."

"Sorry, Madam. I say, Madam, what about a little extra for my trouble today?"

"I beg your pardon?"

"Extra money. I'd like some extra for bringin' the tree in." He held his hand out.

"Nonsense, away with you."

"I must insist, missus." Peter had a very impertinent tone.

"No! Get out now!"

Blaine, your cue, he pleaded silently.

"You heard my Mistress! Be OFF with you!" shouted Blaine in a thunderous voice more suited for a theatre.

Peter's response to this was to kick over a hall table upon which was a vase, of value he hoped. It smashed into smithereens.

"How dare you, brigand, fiend!" Blaine tackled him from behind. Peter slumped to the floor. Mrs. Blaine came and sat heavily upon his back, causing him a sharp pain so that he cried out.

"Oh I am sorry," she whispered, and shifted her bulk a little, causing him even more pain. "Is that better?"

Peter was sure it was all over. But Mrs. Mercer was so occupied screaming for her husband that she did not hear.

In a few minutes, Peter was securely tied with rope.

"Very brave of you, Blaine," said his master, searching Tom's pockets for some reason of his own. Thank God he had thought of removing his badge! He surely would not strip him to his vest!

"What's this?" Mercer whipped out the photo wrapped in the handkerchief.

Oh no, Peter groaned to himself.

"My late mother's likeness, sir, I always carry it, don't man'andle it, please I beg you."

The handkerchief was of poor cotton, so Mercer just threw it aside, and Peter said a silent thanks to God.

"Shall I go for the constable, sir?" Blaine asked. "And I think the Boot Room would be a suitable prison of a temporary nature for this impenitent brigand."

CHAPTER FIFTY-SIX

Eliza had heard the murmur of voices above her window but could not decipher anything. She thought it was Mr. Mercer and Blaine speaking. After a while, she heard shouts from inside the house, and screaming, and then all fell silent. It was getting dark. She had not light enough to work, so she put away her sewing.

The door opened and the Mercers came in. They had a look of vicious intent, and she backed away. Mr. Mercer stepped quickly behind her and grasped her roughly by the arms, forcing her into a chair. She screamed. Mrs. Mercer rummaged on the sewing table.

"This will do," she said, finding a length of calico and tearing it into strips.

"Don't –!" Eliza's cry was cut off by the gag tightly put on her mouth. Then her hands were tied behind the chair. She was helpless. What was going on? Were they going to kill her?

They left. Darkness fell. Eliza, very cold and unable to help herself, her hands tied tightly, moaned in pain.

CHAPTER FIFTY-SEVEN

"Mrs. Blaine, you're shaking." Mrs. Mercer was annoyed to see the tea wobble as it was poured into the cup.

"I'm sorry, Madam. That was a terrible thing that happened this afternoon."

"You didn't look at all frightened at the time, I must say. You looked very calm."

"I won't be easy while he's in the house, Madam. I swept up all the shards. I hope I got them all."

"I hope so too. Look, some of the tea is on the saucer. I hate to see a cup sitting in a puddle of tea."

"I'm sorry, Madam."

Mrs. Blaine did not know what was taking the police so long. Her husband had told her the story – their new employers were murderers and kidnappers – and at the time she had played her part with great enthusiasm. The prisoner 'Tom B' was a famous Liverpool detective! But now she was petrified with terror.

The Mercers had gone together into the still room and she'd heard the girl scream and cry out, and then nothing, and they'd come out again and locked the door, taking the key. When she had asked if she could take Miss Mercer's tea in, Madam had said she wouldn't need it.

The girl was dead! They'd murdered her! That's why she was shaking and the tea was wobbly going into the cups. It was dark and she was alone in the house with two ruthless murderers. Would she be next?

When she came downstairs it occurred to her that she could set the prisoner free if she went about it very quietly. There was another key kept outside under a stone. The Master did not know about this key.

She could not stay in this house for one minute more without protection.

CHAPTER FIFTY-EIGHT

Peter had loosened the ties and was assiduously working himself free. He heard the key in the lock, and the door opened, and Mrs. Blaine come in.

"You had better come out," she whispered, her face white in the light of the candle she carried.

"Are the police here? Help me get free."

"No, but I'm on my own with the murderers!"

"It's only suspicion as yet," he tried to calm her.

"But they murdered the girl. I heard her cry out and then nothing."

"Untie me, quickly!"

She set the candle down and completed the task he had begun, and she led the way to the still room.

Peter was in agony of heart. He was horrified in case this had gone wrong, that his beloved Eliza was dead – that he could not save her!

"They locked the door and took the key," said Mrs. Blaine to him. "There's a connecting door to the ironing room - I know where that key is."

"Hurry, hurry - I beg you!"

She took the candle and fumbled about in a wall cupboard for what seemed like ages, until producing the keys she wanted. She unlocked the ironing room door and led the way to the connecting door. Peter unlocked it and drew back the bolt. She hung back, frightened again, and he took the candle from her.

CHAPTER FIFTY-NINE

Eliza had struggled to get out of the chair, tried to work her way over to the table, to try to somehow get the scissors there. She didn't know what she would do when she got it, it was enough for now to move closer to it. But in trying to move the chair she was tied to, she fell over, and lay, still tied to the chair, on the ground. It was dark now and her tears were spent. She was convinced that she would die. She was very cold and felt herself near death, the gag interfered with the flow of breath, and her nose was a little stuffed, so that her chest heaved in and out with effort.

God help me. I'm going to die. I have to forgive them, don't I? Do I? After all they've done? Very well, before I die I forgive them. All three. And – and that fortune teller. Maybe she knew no better. But what of Peter? He will suffer so much - Lord, send him another to love. I don't want him to be alone and unhappy.

She shut her eyes and slid into semi-consciousness.

She was barely aware that a door opened and that footsteps were coming close. She heard her name called...now someone's hand was on her forehead, and fingertips on her neck.

Peter had set the candle on the floor and quickly felt for the carotid pulse under the jawline. It was beating. He looked about, spied the scissors, and in another moment the gag was cut off and her wrists were free.

"Oh my darling," he said, lifting her and pressing her to his breast. "Eliza, you're alive. You're alive! Mrs. Blaine! Some water, please! Take deep breaths, Eliza."

"It's you!" she managed to say. "They wouldn't let me write, I..."

"Shhh! I know all."

CHAPTER SIXTY

She was on her feet at last. Her hair was undone and tumbled loose about her shoulders.

They heard a loud banging on the front door.

"Can you come upstairs, do you think? I want you to see the arrest." Peter said, after she drank all the water.

"Arrest? Them? Yes, I can."

In the Hall, Mr. Mercer was shouting for Mrs. Blaine.

"Why haven't you answered the door? Where are you, stupid woman?"

He opened the door himself and was surprised to see three constables.

"My, the entire Force," he said. "I am Anthony Mercer, this is my wife, Mrs. Mercer, and the prisoner is in the Boot Room."

"No, I am not," said a voice behind him. He turned in surprise.

"What – how?"

"It's her! She's out!" Mrs. Mercer sped toward the figure of Eliza, who looked like a wraith in the gaslight, thin and pale, her hair tousled about her face.

"Mr. and Mrs. Mercer, attend if you please. I am Detective Constable Peter Reid from Liverpool Police, and you are under arrest for kidnapping," Peter said, showing his badge.

"Reid! What! You! You!" Mr. Mercer shouted. "No, this can't be true!"

"It is true," said one of the constables. "And you and Mrs. Mercer are also wanted under suspicion of murder in Liverpool in the year 1870. I have the warrants here, signed by Detective Chief Inspector Reid of the Liverpool Division. I believe there's a boat with a jagged hole in it."

Mr. Mercer emitted the enraged bull sound again, causing the old servants to shrink backwards.

Mrs. Mercer cried aloud.

"It was all his idea!" she pointed to her husband.

"You, Madam, are also wanted for cruelty to a child, abandoning a child on Christmas Eve of that same year."

"I did not – I never –" she continued to cry as they put her in handcuffs.

"Anybody for a cuppa?" Mrs. Blaine asked in a whisper. "I'm dying for a cuppa. Mr. Blaine? I'm going to heat up some mince pies."

Peter took the cotton package from the floor where it had lain. He pressed it into Elizabeth's hands.

"You will like this," he said. "You will like this very much. Let us go to the kitchen, you need a cuppa and so do I."

CHAPTER SIXTY-ONE

Elizabeth wished to be married on Christmas Day. It was an unusual request and Father looked up the Canon Law books and was delighted to tell her that her wish could be granted. She regained her strength very quickly with food and rest. Margaret gave her her wedding gown as there was no time to make one.

As well as preparing for the Birth of Jesus, this year the Sisters were readying the convent for the marriage ceremony of the child they had taken in so many years before. Elizabeth asked if she could move back in, and they welcomed her with open arms. Mother Maria knelt before her to ask her forgiveness, but Eliza would not have any of that and dropped to her knees too to give the old nun a big hug. Sister Clare's nerves were as bad as any mother of the bride. She worried about invitations, panicked about the veil being too long one day, and too short the next, and feared that poor Elizabeth did not know the mysteries of married life, and she was in no position to tell her. Margaret was summoned the night before the wedding and the two women were closeted together while it was all explained.

"Does marriage frighten her now?" fussed Sister Clare when Margaret came to the parlour for a cup of tea.

"Aunt, she's looking forward to everything about being married," said her niece with a suppressed chuckle.

"I've given her the cross and chain your grandmother left me," said Sister Clare. "The police found it in Miss Langley's apartment, and when Peter saw it, he knew it was mine."

The church was adorned beautifully for Christmas. Elizabeth and Peter were married in a quiet ceremony late in the afternoon, and a hundred candles cast golden glows on the happy couple. They came out of the church to a guard of honour formed by Peter's colleagues. A very special guest was re-introduced to the new Mrs. Reid, her old nurse Bridie, who marvelled at how grown up and beautiful her little charge was now, the image of her mother!

The Reids gave a large donation to the nuns, and bought a good house in Knotty Ash with a large garden and meadows beyond. There, Mrs. Reid began a sanctuary for injured and abused animals, while Detective Constable Reid – soon to be Inspector – continued his work on the Force. Scotland Yard made him a tempting offer, but he had no desire to leave Liverpool. He and Elizabeth had six children. She rejoiced in her family and made sure they knew how hard life was for many children by taking them to the Refuge regularly. All but the littlest ones attended Midnight Mass at St. Clement's and they knew the story of their Mamma being found on the steps that Christmas Eve a long time ago.

Thank you so much for reading. We hope you really enjoyed the story. Please consider leaving a positive review on Amazon if you did.

WOULD YOU LIKE FREE BOOKS EVERY
WEEK FROM PUREREAD?

Click Here and sign up to receive PureRead updates so we can send them to you each and every week.

Much love, and thanks again,

Your Friends at PureRead